*The Phoenix Saga Continues...*

*Four months after the Classtoria returns with Phoenix to the Hyperion sun system and the planet Darlon, Captain Terry Dankin is assigned his first research mission. But what was supposed to be a simple mission to explore biological and geological aspects of the planet Varasay, the Phoenix runs headlong into an ancient enemy and planetary harvesters, the Parakon. The same enemy that destroyed Captain Darlon's homeworld of Shaleen over twelve hundred years ago.*

*Bent on harvesting planetary resources to strengthen their vast empire in order to protect a mysterious blue, hyper-dwarf star, the Parakon set their sites on Phoenix.*

*Captain Dankin on the* Phoenix, *with the aide of Captain Narell aboard the Heraway, fight off a Parakon scout ship, but then are suddenly faced with the massive and powerful mothership, the Kloose.*

*Despite being greatly outgunned and outsized, Captain Dankin and his crew aboard the Phoenix must insure the Kloose is destroyed before the Parakon find, and harvest, his new home, Darlon.*

# The Pilgrimage of the Phoenix

## Part 2: Parakon

ISBN-13: 978-1482656275

ISBN-10: 1482656272

For my father, Larry Smith.
Thanks for all the bedtime stories as a kid, and proofreading my own stories forty years later!

*Forward*

*Year 1, Day 1, Hyperion Sun System*
*Quadrant Omega-Four of the Milky Way Galaxy*

    *The battered and almost derelict warship* LMS Thunderwalker *entered the Hyperion system at one half the speed of light. The on-board computer system preformed numerous planetary breaking maneuvers before navigating to the fourth planet, then slipped the crescent-shaped ship into a comfortable orbit. After days of scans and readings of the surface conditions, it decided to wake the senior crew, starting with Captain Darlon.*
    *The captain floated dreamless in his fluid-filled Cryo-Chamber. At over eight feet tall, he occupied the largest of the four chambers in the small, darkened room. Soon the gray, viscous fluid began to drain and revealed the heavily bearded*

man dressed in a simple white robe.

While the tank drained, overhead lights flickered on, heaters began to warm the air and computer terminals came to life. Soft beeps emitted as computer programs booted up and came on line.

Once the tank was drained, the computer sent several electrical jolts into the body of the supine captain. Meant to stimulate the diaphragm, it had its desired effect and the captain violently exhaled a murky gray fluid. With arms stiff from a long period of disuse, the captain pulled himself up and leaned over the edge of the chamber, exhaling more fluid onto the cold steel floor.

"Ughh!" he exclaimed and took a deep, gasping breath. His diaphragm fluttered again and more fluid was expelled. For another full minute the captain was racked with heaves and coughs. "Memnos, please tell me this is the last time I have to wake up like this!"

"It is Captain," the computer replied.

Captain Darlon continued to lean outward, gray fluid dripping from his beard. With cold fingers he wiped slime from his eyes. "We have reached the Hyperion System?" His deep voice echoed through the room.

"We have Captain."

The Captain nodded again as he closed his eyes and

*concentrated on breathing while still leaning outside the tank. His white robe stuck to his dark skin with residual fluid, which was getting colder by the second. "Our long range scans were correct?" he asked, coughing.*

*"Yes captain, the planet is habitable and there are no dominant species that would suffer from our population of the surface."*

*Still coughing, the captain slowly climbed from his chamber and disrobed once his feet were on the deck. The soaked fabric fell to the deck with a wet slap. He cleared his throat and spat on the floor. "By the Goddess Miramma that stuff tastes horrid  How long was the voyage?" he asked, carefully making his way to a shower stall on stiff, unsteady legs.*

*"One hundred seventy two years."*

*The captain pressed several buttons and steaming water sprayed from an overhead system. "Senior staff?" he asked aloud.*

*"They will be awaking shortly."*

*"Crew?"*

*"All three hundred crew are safe and sleeping."*

*"Ship?"*

*"Two engines failed during the voyage, but we were already at cruising speed. Hull integrity on decks eight through ten are critical but stable. Deck nine is sealed due to a hull*

breech. Hyronn cannons are offline, but other weapons are operable. Hull shielding down to fifteen percent. Severe fire damage to the bridge, cargo hold six and engineering."

Captain Darlon took all this in as gray fluid washed from his massive frame and down the drain. Normally trying to recall memories after such a long CryoSleep was difficult. Not so this time.

"She took a beating Memnos."

"Yes, Captain."

Finished washing the captain simply stood in the hot water, remembering. The Parakon had come faster than anyone had thought, and better armed. Even still, the Shaleen Alliance had held their own. At least for a while.

The Thunderwalker was by far the most powerful ship of the Alliance, and the sheer carnage she'd doled out on the Parakon was terrifying, eventually taking down twenty four of their vessels single-handedly and damaging dozens of others. But in the end the overwhelming opposition forced the Thunderwalker to retreat to the Gorshev Nebula for repairs. By the time repairs were completed several days later however, the remaining Alliance ships had been destroyed and the planet of Shaleen had been taken. Already were the antigrav laser platforms being placed into orbit.

Captain Darlon initially wanted a final run on the

Parakon, but his responsibility to three hundred crew came first. "It would be a suicide run, Captain," Sub-Captain Hessing had explained and, after three days of passionate council, the decision was made to travel to the Hyperion System. It was known that the fourth planet was habitable, as long range scans verified. The council was fraught with emotion as many still had family back on Shaleen.

"I am open to suggestions," the Captain said on more than one occasion.

"We should run a rescue mission, get as many as we can off the planet!" cried one junior officer.

The Captain grievously shook his head. "The Thunderwalker *is already at maximum occupancy.*"

"And besides," Sub-Captain Hessing broke in, "we'd never make it to the surface. At last scan the Parakon had over a hundred warships in orbit. We would be swarmed and obliterated."

"We can't just do nothing!" someone shouted from the back of the room.

"We aren't," the Captain said calmly, "we are saving ourselves, our culture, our knowledge and our future. We can rebuild in the Hyperion System. Our scans tell us there is a habitable planet there."

The arguments continued for days, but in the end,

*reasoning, sadly, won the day.*

  *The* Thunderwalker *used the cover of the nebula to escape Parakon sensors and set course. Captain Darlon felt as if he were running from a fight as he stood stoically on the war-torn bridge and watched Shaleen, his home planet, fall farther and farther away.*

  *Still standing in the steaming water, the captain asked, "No trace of Parakon pursuit?"*

  *"None Captain," Memnos replied.*

  *"Any other space faring occupants in this sector?"*

  *"Negative."*

  *"Does the planet have a satellite?"*

  *"Yes, a stable class seven moon. It will serve well as an outpost and base of operations."*

  *The captain finished rinsing and touched another button. A small panel opened and he retrieved a small laser device. Activating it, he waved it over his face and head and wet mats of hair fell to the shower floor.*

  *Now bald and beardless, the captain stepped from the shower, dried and retrieved his uniform from a nearby locker. While he dressed he was occasioned by his command team awaking behind him, gagging and hurling CryoWater explosively.*

  *"People, people! Show a little decorum shall we and gag a little quieter? I'm trying to think!"*

"His Majesty has spoken my fellow subjects," Sub-Captain Merall Hessing proclaimed.

"And you Sub-Captain! In your chamber without a garment? Is it your wish for us to see you naked and slimy?"

Hessing climbed shakily from his tank and looked down at his own nakedness. "I thought you would be rather flattered Captain." While not as tall as the captain, Hessing was still an imposing figure. From the forest-choked North Continent of the planet Hyloph, his skin was carbon-gray, making his orange eyes stand out even more. He was a powerful man with a keen sense of intellect. Captain Darlon had chosen him out of three hundred candidates for the Sub-Captain position aboard Thunderwalker. He had never regretted the decision.

"Rest assured, I am anything but flattered Sub-Captain," the captain said while buttoning his uniform blazer. His uniform, like all senior officers, was midnight-blue and adorned only with his rank; two interlocking silver circles at the center of his chest.

"How about you Sub-Commander Quell? Are you flattered?"

"Not in the least Captain. In fact, I'm a little nauseated by it," Seng Quell said while wringing slime from his own beard. He coughed repeatedly and spit phlegm onto the steel decking. "By the gods I hate waking up like this."

The last to emerge from his tank was First Officer Perrell

9

*Reller. Reller and Quell were also from Hyloph, but from the South Continent, a sparse and demanding land. They too had carbon-gray skin, but were much shorter in stature than the Sub-Captain.*

*"How about you Mr. Reller? Are you impressed with the Sub-Captain's manhood flapping in the wind?" the captain joked. He adjusted the cuffs of his uniform before attaching a communications device to his forearm.*

*"With all due respect Captain, I refuse to get pulled into a discussion concerning my Sub-Captains' manhood flapping in the non-existent wind. My intellect demands that anyone's manhood flapping in the wind is a pointless and futile discussion," Reller answered.*

*"Be that as it may, I am still not impressed Sub-Captain. Now all three of you hairy animals, please wash, dress and meet me on the bridge."*

*"We are at Hyperion System?" the Sub-Captain asked.*

*Barbs and joking ceased as the the senior crew members looked up at the captain. "Yes," he explained, "and the planet is habitable. We have a new home gentlemen. It's year one, day one and we've a lot of work to do."*

*The three officers went about their showers as the captain left the CryoRoom. "Memnos?" he asked while leaving the room and entering a long hallway, his heavy boots clanging on the gridiron floor.*

*"Yes, Captain?"*

*"Wake second tier officers please. Also please ready two shuttle craft, I'd like to go to the surface as soon as possible."*

*"Yes, Captain."*

*"Oh, and one last thing."*

*"Yes?"*

*"Thank you for keeping us safe."*

*"You're welcome Captain."*

* * *

*Year 2, Hyperion Sun System, Planet Darlon*
*Quadrant Omega-Four of the Milky Way Galaxy*

*The first war with the Parakon was decisive in favor of Shaleen. The Parakon had come for the unique and plentiful mineral resources of the planet, minerals that could be processed quickly to build more Parakon warships and weapons for their ongoing war with anyone who would take their blue star. They came without warning, without greeting, only brute force. Had it not been for the powerful Darlon family guiding the Shaleen into a highly successful space-faring civilization, the Parakon would have easily conquered the planet on the first raid.*

*Captain Ashek Darlon, having no interest in family politics or a desk job, chose a path that led him to starship captaincy. That choice, in the end, led him to be the lone surviving member of the Darlon family.*

*Yet despite the ultimate defeat of the Shaleen Alliance, a panel of senior officers aboard* Thunderwalker *met and unanimously ratified the naming of their new world as Darlon. The captain was not aware of this secret vote, but was honored by their decision.*

*"You humble me. I took a different path from the rest of my family, including my brother. I despised politics and wanted nothing to do with high-profile. Yet even I cannot deny the impact my family had on our people, our survival of the first Parakon attack."*

*During the first year it was agreed that the Shaleen government would be adopted for Darlon. The Captain himself appointed members of his senior crew to government positions until a formal election could be held. Sub-Captain Hessing was appointed the first President. "That should be your position Captain. You are the leader of this crew," he'd said grudgingly. He and the captain were standing on a small grassy rise outside of Quell, the first town to be built. A wide, slow river ran behind them, through a forest and ultimately to the sea. The river was already proving to be a primary source of travel and*

*transportation. Despite the available technology on*
Thunderwalker, *it was still going to take many generations to*
*reach the advancement of Shaleen.*

*"I am still the captain of* Thunderwalker, *President*
*Hessing, my first obligation is to said ship. She is still in need of*
*repairs. And besides, I will also be overseeing the building of a*
*base on our moon. We need to be ready." The captain looked up*
*at the nearly-full moon. Named Phrass for the Shaleen goddess of*
*light, its brightness this evening was already so strong as to cast*
*shadows in the twilight. Around the men's legs a cool breeze*
*waved through the rusty-red grass.*

*Hessing wrinkled his brow. "For what? This sector of*
*space is vacant for light years in every direction."*

*The captain was nodding. "That is true, but what the*
*Parakon did to us, to others –," he broke off before continuing.*
*They may never find us here, but still, we must be ready if they, or*
*someone else, does."*

*A year later, Quell was a bustling city. Couples bonded*
*and children were born. Cities rose and commerce flourished.*
*Fishermen took to the plentiful seas and farmers took to the*
*vibrant lands. Schools were built in anticipation of future*
*children. Infrastructure was established and planetary defenses*
*were erected.*

*Captain Darlon rarely returned to the surface. Occupied*

with extensive repairs to Thunderwalker *and directing extra-planetary defenses and asteroid harvesting, he rarely had time to visit the colonies and his former senior officers.*

*But on the sixteenth month of the Darlon occupation, a dedication was held at the ocean's edge, just two miles from Quell. Most of the city put work aside and stood quietly in the gray sand to listen to Captain Darlon as he mounted a small stage. Next to him stood a thick, two meter high column with a marble-carved planet on top. The replica of Shaleen was almost a meter in diameter.*

*The Captain took a breath and began to speak, then stopped. He looked at the pre-written speech in his hands for a moment, then looked to his left, out over the ocean and the morning sun. Slowly he folded the paper and returned it to a small pocket in his uniform blazer.*

*"To us," he began, his deep, gravelly voice carrying over the crowd before him, "only sixteen months have passed since our flight from Shaleen, but in reality it has been three generations."* *He paused for a moment, still looking out over the rolling surf and the ocean beyond. "Perhaps we will never know what has become of our homeworld, and though it pains me to say, perhaps we should not ask," his voice trailed off softly.*

*The eight foot commander of the* Thunderwalker *then looked out over the crowd before him. "We came here as four different races from four different planets, but already those races are blurred and are becoming one. We are no longer Shaleen, or Hyloph, or Gheld or even Therak. We are now Darlonians, and this is our home.*

*"But we must never forget where we came from, nor forget those who died; our families, children and friends. Today we honor their memories, though a marble statue hardly seems fitting. What is fitting is that we remember them, remember our home and honor our roots in the cosmos.*

*"We are here but for a fleeting moment and we should remember the past, but not dwell in it. Our future is bright here on this new world. If we lay the path before us with integrity and principle, then future generations will look back on us with pride and honor. Let us not let them down. Let us build a world, a culture, a society they will flourish in. Let us be true. Let us be honest. Let us lay a path to the future with gold, so our past will always shine. My words are simple and small, but together our actions speak of who we are.*

*"Today we dedicate this sculpture to the memory of Shaleen and all our peoples, but I also ask that as we build for the future, keep them in your hearts as well," the Captain finished.*

*A raucous round of applause followed him off the stage. President Hessing greeted him with a handshake. "Well said*

*Captain."*

*"Thank you Mr. President."*

*"I wish you'd call me Merall."*

*"Would you call me Ashek if I asked you?" the captain responded with a smile.*

*"I would not," the President replied with an equal smile. The two men walked to the nearby, small runner-ship that would take the captain back to* Thunderwalker. *When they arrived they shook hands again.*

*"Well wishes and safe flight Captain," President Hessing expressed.*

*"Well wishes to you also my friend," the captain replied, then looked back towards the villagers. Some stood in small groups chatting amongst themselves while most departed. "They respect you, as do I. You've done a extraordinary job." He turned back towards his one-time sub-captain. "May the gods of Telarr continue to bless you."*

*"And you as well Captain." They shared a quick embrace before the captain boarded the runner-ship.*

*Smiling, Captain Darlon watched the town of Quell grow smaller as the ship rose through the morning sky. "We have come so far and our future is bright with promise, so bright," he said quietly to himself.*

Planet Darlon

Darlon Year 1272


"Driver, home please, Terry Dankin," I said, climbing aboard a specially modified orbit-to-surface zephyr. As I settled back into the seat that morphed to my body shape the door locked with a *chunk* sound, the interior pressurized and, slowly, the zephyr moved down a launch tunnel. After passing through a field barrier a small hatch opened beneath the little two man pod, exposing the vacuum of space. With the assistance of a shot of compressed air, the zephyr was then gently shot through a small launch tube and out into open space.

Darlon's immense gravity did the rest.

Even after several months of this trip back to the surface of Darlon, it still left me unsettled. A zephyr looks like an elongated egg, with antigravity pads on the bottom and, in case of an emergency, a parachute tucked away in the roof cone. There were literally millions of zephyrs in service and to my knowledge, a parachute emergency had never happened. Every zephyr in the fleet was monitored by a single AI computer called Zephyr Command, and when even the tiniest issues was recorded, the zephyr was sent for repairs.

There's not much to a zephyr, and dropping from over a hundred fifty kilometers can, well, make my stomach want nothing but crackers and water for the next few hours as it tries to dislodge itself from the back of my throat. Jhenna found the trip exhilarating. Me, not so much. At least I could now make the trip without having to opaque the window. Sometimes I would look up and watch the Orbital Research Ring fade away into the distance. It was, after all, easier watching something really big move *away* from you than watch a planet move *towards* you, at a high rate of speed I might add.

Actually, the plummet to the surface wasn't too bad, until you reentered the atmosphere. Then the swaying and jerking through the turbulence left the whole experience with something to be desired. But, slowly, I'd been getting used to it.

Bringing along some reading material to occupy myself for the forty minute trip home helped as well. My current study was a book called "Darlon and the Hyperion System: Twelve

Hundred Years in the Making," by Un Pal Het, one of the foremost historians on the planet. The reading was a bit dry and monotone, but fascinating nonetheless. As the zephyr took me home, I flipped to the chapter where Pal Het theorizes on the remarkable fact that Darlon has never seen a war. The occasional skirmish, sure, but they were small and resolved quickly. His current hypothesis was that because so many people on Darlon had seen worlds and civilizations crumble, including some of their own, they realize the importance of peace, equality and stability in government and culture. I read on as we entered the upper atmosphere.

My assigned home was on the continent of Ohwehoss overlooking the Arion Sea. It was a small, but comfortable home who's nearest neighbors were over a kilometer away. There were no roads coming or going to the home; in fact, there were no roads anywhere on Darlon. Everything was transported by zephyrs, or some modified versions of them. The burning of fossil fuels, of which Darlon was rich in, was strictly forbidden, so no internal combustion engines powered any other type of vehicle.

The zephyr eventually dropped through thick cloud cover and, as the Plummet of Death, as I used to call it, began to slow, I could see my home in the distance, perched on the edge of a twenty-story cliff. The sun was just setting as I sailed in over the tree tops and slowly lowered to the ground. After parking the zephyr in its docking cradle, I entered my home at the point of total exhaustion.

"Evening Coeus," I said aloud to my personal AI.

"Greetings Terry, how was the graduation?"

"Fun, with a bit of crazy on the side."

Putting my newly minted degree aside, I stripped to my skivvies, donned a robe and deposited my dirty clothing into the clothing vacuum. They would be sucked to the nearest laundry facility for cleaning and pressing. From my understanding the nearest cleaning facility was twenty kilometers away, but somehow my clothes made it there, were cleaned, then returned to my home within thirty hours. Pretty darned convenient. My mother would have loved a system like this, it would have made raising five sons a bit easier. I pressed a button and my ball of clothing was sucked away with a whoosh.

Retrieving a bottle of water and an almost empty bag of crackers, I plopped myself down in a living room chair and looked through bay windows and out over the Arion Sea. Sail ships cruised by at leisure as the setting sun rippled its golden glory off the endless turquoise waters. Darlon was indeed a beautiful planet, resplendent with blue and green and clean air and humid warmth. The bay far below my home was alive with bird life and leaping fish, and the coastline was overwhelmed with flowering bushes of every imaginable color.

Just off my front porch, an open-air elevator led down to a beach at the bottom of the cliff. It was a beautiful, secluded and peaceful place to relax, but I'd been so busy with studying I'd only been down twice.

It had been four months since our return to the Darlonian system aboard *Classtoria*. Upon our return Commander Ballon strongly suggested I put myself through several command classes at the Darlonian Space Exploration Administration (DSEA), and I jumped at the chance.

"Bring yourself up to speed with our laws and procedures," he explained. "You'll need to if you wish your ship to be part of DSEA. And besides, I always need new captains at my beck and call," he finished with a smile.

What followed was four intense and brutal months of book study on everything from common law and administration to hands-on classes that included ship-based weapons systems. I would frequently wake up in the middle of the night still in uniform and paperwork all over the bed. It was grueling.

But finally I graduated, Commander Ballon doing the honors of presenting me with my full captaincy papers. I was now approved to take on assigned missions of exploration with *Phoenix*. "Four months?" Jhenna had asked. She'd been at my graduation as well. "What took so long?" She, of course, only had to download all the books and information, which took all of seven seconds.

"Careful," I'd told her, "I'll demote you to the zephyr maintenance crew."

Jhenna and I had become very close over the last few months. I'd contacted her many times with questions about a set of laws or regulations, or questions about antigrav technology. Sometimes she would come to my home and, at my request, give me verbal pop-quizzes on whatever I was currently studying.

Or sometimes we wouldn't talk about my classes at all and, instead, discuss the Moonbase Ronald Reagan survivors. Two older survivors had passed away within months of our return to Darlon, their passing attributed to old age, but the rest slowly began to integrate into their new lives. Even Michael Lehay, the one time governor of MRR had found a calling. Discovering a love of all the different languages present on Darlon, he set out to study and learn as many as he could, his eventual goal to become a language professor at a university.

And sometimes Jhenna and I would just sit on my porch and look out over the Arion Sea and discuss her continuing understanding of emotions and what they meant. Since her raw data was based on human-based programming and information, I was her logical go-to person when she had questions; she needed a human to ask about human emotions.

There were several emotions she struggled with, one of

them being anger and/or frustration. Of all the other independent AI's (there were only eight), she was the only one with such advanced emotions and she found working with them, at times, to be frustrating. "I find that sometimes emotions and gut feelings are important to making a decision," she once said, "but to my contemporaries, it is illogical. I have a difficult time trying to express why I feel one way or another."

On one such occasion, when she had proposed a solution to a problem, a colleague had asked her how she'd arrived at such a conclusion. Her only answer was to shrug and say, "My feelings tell me this is the logical answer," and her solution was rejected for another. Later in the formulation process it was discovered that Jhenna's original answer was correct, yet she received no apology or recognition. On that particular day she showed up at my home unannounced, in tears. "My eyes are burning and leaking!" she'd exclaimed. "I fear some part of me is malfunctioning!" She was a complete wreck.

She'd arrived at my home via a zephyr, which had fallen over in the front yard. If you don't dock a zephyr properly before shutting it down, they simply fall to the ground and roll onto their sides. But I only smiled and, saying nothing, stepped forward and embraced her. She returned the embrace and cried on my chest for a full two minutes before she composed herself.

Which brought up her second emotional struggle, love.

Once she'd composed herself somewhat, she pushed back slightly, leaned her head back, stood on her tip toes and kissed me. Caught off-guard, I reciprocated for a moment, then gently pulled away. "This is not a solution to what you feel," I found myself saying, though I felt disappointment in my own words. Jhenna and I had become close and even I had some romantic thoughts, but as I was her captain and she my first officer, I felt it inappropriate. Perhaps that was a lame excuse, or perhaps not. In my mind, in my reality, I was only four months separate from Ressa, and with my memories still coming back little by little, I felt uncomfortable with my emotions for Jhenna. My long-ago wife was still too fresh in my mind.

Though I felt guilt, Jhenna seemed to understand. "My apologies Captain, I – am still struggling to understand." To that I only smiled and hugged her again.

Over the next few months, we met only in a professional manner. We continued to discuss her emotions, as well as other things, but we kept it platonic. I would be lying if I said I didn't think of Jhenna in a romantic sense; after all, she knew me better than anyone would, but until I accepted my own emotions concerning Ressa, my feelings for her would have to take a back seat.

So Jhenna continued to help me with my studies, even though we both felt an underlying attraction. She'd helped me all the way through the final testing without complaint, always happy to help coach and guide me through the information.

But, now, it was over with and I was home. As I watched the ships sail far below, I thought of her dedication in helping me with my classwork. But there was a part of me that didn't know if her dedication to helping me learn was because of a professional obligation, or because of her personal feeling towards me.

I shook my thoughts clear and called out, "Any communications for me Coeus?"

"In fact, Terry, one just arrived. And I must say, I am still uncomfortable calling you Terry."

"I know Coeus, just humor me. Calling me Captain when I'm sitting here in a robe in my own home is just too formal. On *Phoenix* it's Captain, here it's Terry."

"Very well. The message is from DSEA and is lengthy, would you like the abridged version?"

"Please."

After a momentary pause, "You are being assigned your first mission. It is a geological, and hopefully biological expedition to the planet Varasay in the Kaperkis Sector."

I raised my eyebrows. "That was fast. Perhaps I should hear the whole message." Coeus played the entire message for me, which took almost ten minutes. When complete, I asked Coeus to contact Jhenna. She was currently writing new computer programs that would increase jump ring efficiency for all of the DSEA deep space starship fleet. And by deep, I mean traveling to other galaxies, not just within the Milky Way. Darlonian ships regularly visited other galaxies already, but it currently took months worth of jumps to get there, even for *Classtoria*. Jhenna and her team were writing programs that would hopefully cut the time in half. When she chimed in on my comm pad, I answered with a visual connection and smiled.

"Greetings Cap –, I mean Terry. What can I do for you?" she asked.

"First Officer Jhenna, how would you like to take a little trip? The *Phoenix* has been assigned her first mission."

## 2

Darlon Year 1272

Aboard DS *Phoenix*

The voice of Jhenna came over the comm speakers and echoed in the biggest cargo-hold of the *Phoenix*. "Captain?"

I laid down a wrench that was too small and picked up a larger one. "Yes?" I said aloud.

"We are on final approach to Varasay. Estimated final orbit insertion in just under two hours."

"Very well, thank you." I looked at the wrench in my greasy hands, then placed it back in its tray. Work on my custom zephyr would have to wait. At least I'd gotten the bucket seats installed and the exterior painting done; dark red with black accents. I'd also painted the *Phoenix* logo on the front, for no other reason than it looked good.

Jhenna was perplexed as to why I would want to customize my own zephyr; they were readily available on Darlon, the Orbital Rings and every ship in the Darlonian fleet. But I found the hands-on work satisfying. In 2090, when I was eight years old, my father and I rebuilt a 2052 Ford Aileron, one of the first hovercars ever made. I loved the smell and feel of grease on my hands; the clanking of metal tools.

Best of all, it kept me occupied. Our four day voyage to Varasay included a lot of down time, so I had a standard surface to orbit zephyr brought aboard before departure. My hands had been covered in synthetic grease pretty much ever since.

But, I thought as I put my tools away, the call to duty is never far away. Once the last wrench was secured I looked around the cargo bay. Much had changed aboard the *Nations Ship Phoenix,* now rechristened *D. S. (Darlon Starship) Phoenix,* in the four months since we'd returned to the Darlonian system. All equipment and gear originally intended for the mission to Dione was removed, new hardware and storage lockers were installed. A small sickbay was built as well as an engineering office. Personal living quarters were also built, though they were small. Plumbing was installed as well to handle the showering stalls and sinks throughout the ship. We even had a commissary built for longer voyages to accommodate hungry bellies of twenty crew members.

The commissary was my idea. Other smaller ships just had

small vending cubicles, but I wanted something more homey and comfortable; a place where people could gather in small groups, sit in comfortable chairs and talk over real food, not freeze-dried food in plastic-wrapped boxes.

Captain Laylop, the recently promoted primary engineer behind the reconfiguration and refitting of *Phoenix*, was a bit perplexed at first, but once the plans came together he became quite a proponent, and his design was marvelous. It wasn't overly spacious, but it was comfortable, seated up to fifteen people, and we even had our own chef. Chef Boonod, from the planet Erons, was a tall, thin man with unusually long fingers, big coal-black eyes and a warm and kind demeanor. His take on food was like an artist with paint and canvas and he was able to cook a variety of foods from many, many worlds. The Chefs circular food prep area was in the middle of the room. You placed your order then stood and watched as it was prepared. It became quite popular with many on board to gather just to watch him work his magic with long dextrous fingers. Mealtimes aboard *Phoenix* were cherished by all.

But the ultimate addition was that *Phoenix* now had her own jump ring. It wasn't as powerful as *Classtoria's* ring, but we could still cover many light years in a single jump. The *Classtoria* could have jumped to Varasay in a single jump, but *Phoenix* took four days; a total of thirty seven light years.

Still, I didn't mind, it was nice to have the down time and just be a regular person for a while, especially after my rigorous four month training classes. "Coeus?" I called out while wiping grease and paint from my hands.

"Yes, Captain?"

"Please inform the Chef Boonod that I'd like to have a BLT and green tea for lunch. I'll be there in about twenty minutes."

"Very well, Captain."

Fifteen minutes later I was showered, in a fresh uniform and headed towards the commissary. On the way I ran into my newest engineer, Veresh. She came from a little-known sector of the Milky Way galaxy called the Donnor Sector, an area on the very edge of the galaxy that was highly isolated. Because of this isolation, her people became highly advanced space farers and eventually became trading partners with Darlon.

Though quiet most of the time, she was exceptionally intelligent. With wide reddish eyes and a high forehead, she carried herself with dignity and pride. Currently she was designing a permanent shuttle craft, named *P.S. Odyssey*, for the *Phoenix*. We had temporary transport zephyrs, but they fit awkwardly into the new hanger deck, as well as took up too much space. The new *P.S. Odyssey* would dock to the underside of *Phoenix*.

"Hello Lieutenant," I greeted.

"Greetings Captain. How is the zephyr retrofit going?"

"Well enough I guess, but I'm having problems with the steering modulator."

She looked perplexed for a moment. "Why would you need to adjust the steering modulators?"

I smiled. "I'm prone to motion sickness, so I'm trying to alter the steering so it doesn't take such drastic directional changes."

"I see. That does make sense. Do you require assistance?"

"Not yet, I'm not one to let a bag of bolts defeat me."

Veresh cocked her head. "Bag of bolts, sir?"

Smiling again, I replied, "Just a figure of speech. How's *Odyssey* coming along?

She motioned to a specialized blueprint tablet computer in her hand. "The blueprints are done. We have one last review meeting next week. After that, construction begins."

"Sounds good, you did get the cup holder for the captain's chair, right?"

It was now Veresh's turn to smile. "Not only that, but the holder will come equipped with a warmer and chiller."

We parted ways and I made my way to the commissary, but not before stopping at a small memorial in the corridor. Mounted in a frame on the wall was the *Phoenix* logo flanked by the two mission ID tags of my crewmembers, Yuri Korapov and Michelle Harishi; their faces smiling. My faded memories, caused by over two hundred years in the BioChamber aboard *Phoenix*, had slowly returned over the months. The most painful being memories of my wife, and a son I'd never met, but also of Michelle and Yuri. Just about every day brought back a memory or two; some funny, some poignant, a few bringing a tear to my eyes, all making me catch my breath.

I reached up and lightly touched the glass covering. I'd originally thought to have a burial in space for my friends, but once I saw the beauty of Darlon I decided instead on a mausoleum near my home. Along with their names on their side by side plaques, the words 'Welcome Home" were also engraved. The ceremony was short and private, attended by only Jhenna and myself. I only said a few small prayers because, well, I didn't know really what else to do or say, but I hoped that was enough.

Looking at the two smiling faces of my long ago friends, I found myself smiling, then headed off for lunch.

My sandwich and tea awaited me as ordered, but Jhenna also awaited me. "I thought we'd go over the mission parameters again while you dined," she said from a nearby table.

I nodded my approval, grabbed my sandwich and tea and joined her at the table. Varasay was unique in that its surface was over ninety-five percent water. There were no major land masses, only long chains of volcanic islands. Even more unique was that no ocean was deeper than two hundred meters. Long range scans also told us that Varasay had no moon and was one of only three planets orbiting their sun, Seld. Other than that, not much was known, hence the exploratory mission by *Phoenix*.

Jhenna and I discussed some of the mission details while I ate my sandwich. Two satellites were to be placed in orbit, one polar, the other sun-synchronous, not only to map the shallow bottom and volcanic islands, but to observe future island development. Two solar powered submarines were also to be deployed to study water conditions, temperatures, salinity and a host of other aspects, including the search for life, if it wasn't already obvious when we arrived.

Two other satellites were also to be deployed around Varasay's planetary neighbors, Herra and Vista. Herra was the inner-most world, a scorched little planet of rock and dust. Vista was the outer-most world, a gas giant composed mostly of hydrogen and helium. Its tremendous mass suggested that there may have once been other planets in the system, but Vista had consumed them. Not much was expected to be discovered from Herra and Vista as they were typical finds in most solar systems.

But Varasay was different and everyone aboard was excited about its exploration. Even Mr. Or, temporarily borrowed from the *Classtoria*, was giddy with excitement. "It is rare to find such a world so dominated by water," he'd said. A HoloTable had been installed for him on the bridge and he was anxious to start studying the planet. He was predicting abundant life in the planetary ocean. "Every form of life we've ever discovered depends on water, Varasay is bound to be overflowing with life of all sorts!" His excitement was infectious.

Jhenna and I concluded our meeting, departed the commissary and made our way to the bridge. Once there I asked Coeus for an update.

"Approaching for final orbital insertion now Captain."

"Do we have a visual?"

"Yes, Captain."

I sat back in my chair and punched a small button. The facetless diamond window went from opaque to clear in a matter of seconds and revealed a breathtaking site. Before us laid a brilliantly blue world that seemed to glow from within. Banks of white clouds drifted over the blue seas and at the poles, white ice caps could be seen. On the horizon, the thin layer of atmosphere glowed like a blue halo.

Mr. Or came onto the bridge at that point and stopped, transfixed by the view. "Oh my..." he said, then moved off to his station. He quickly brought a hologram of Varasay up and began studying lines of code. "Goodness!" he exclaimed.

"What is it Mr. Or?" I asked.

"Life, Captain, life everywhere!" he said with an immense smile. He swiped his hand over the hologram and enlarged a particular area. I rose from my chair and joined him. There, in the glowing blue waters, massive schools of fish-like creatures swam in synchronicity towards the shoreline of a small volcanic island. The island was dotted with green. Mr. Or swiped again and focused on a large, moving patch of green out on the open water. "A floating forest?" he asked to himself. "The hydroponic aspects must be fascinating!"

I returned to my chair and marveled at the view while Coeus brought us into orbit. As we got closer, numerous island chains came into view, most of them volcanic-black, but some were green with vegetation. And there were more of those peculiar floating forests that undulated with each sea swell that rolled under them. I touched a button on my comm pad. "Dr. Wesh?"

"Captain?" came the reply.

"We are now at Varasay and Mr. Or has discovered the planet is quite full of life."

"Not to worry Captain, the subs have already been through their sterilization processes. There'll be no organism transference."

"Very well, thank you." The DSEA had extremely strict guidelines when it came to exploring other planets. Chief among them was eliminating any possibility of transferring organisms from ship to surface, or vice versa. Even after landing on a new world, all exits from the ship had to be sealed with field barriers and those leaving the ship had to wear protective suits, even if the air was breathable. In other words, it was nothing like the science fiction movies of my youth.

"Coeus?"

"Yes, Captain?"

"Once orbit has been achieved, please prepare to disengage the jump ring." Since landing could not be achieved with the jump ring mag locked to the ship, it was disengaged and left in orbit.

"Captain," Jhenna said from the engineers chair, "I've located a suitable island for landing. It's approximately two kilometers long, most of it flat from lava flow. The occupying volcano is dormant."

I nodded. "Sounds like a plan. Mr. Or, how's the surface?"

The science officer waved his four arms in a practiced cadence and brought up holographic lines of computer code. "Air is breathable, mostly nitrogen and oxygen. Temperature at the equator averages ninety degrees and minus twenty at the poles. Gravity is eighty-five percent of Darlon. Oceans are highly saline with a touch of sulfur as well."

Varasay now took up the entire viewing window as Coeus

cut in with an update. "Stable orbit achieved, preparing to disengage jump ring." After a moment, several vibrations could be felt through the bridge flooring. "Mag locks terminated."

"Jhenna, would you back us off a bit?" I asked.

Jhenna touched a few controls to slow the *Phoenix* down ever so slightly. Soon the elliptical jump ring appeared through the bridge window and began fading off into the distance. We'd practiced this maneuver in orbit around Darlon several times, but this time felt a little different. "Don't lose it Coeus, that's our ticket home," I said.

"I'll do my best, sir."

I called down to engineering to insure the satellites were ready for launch. After an affirmative I turned and spoke, "They're all yours Mr. Or."

The science officer nodded, then replaced the hologram of Varasay with one of the *Phoenix*. He typed in several commands and two, small orbs ejected from the side of the ship. After a moment, micro-engines kicked on and the satellites moved off in different directions. For several minutes Mr. Or sent a battery of communications tests to the little robots, then smiled. "It will take several days for them to reach their proper orbits, but communications and maneuvering test perfect."

"Very good," I said and turned to Jhenna. "Jhenna, as you are the First Officer, Chief Engineer and Chief Pilot, I'll allow you to give yourself your own orders about getting to the surface."

"How very courteous of you Captain."

"Yes, I know. I like empowering my underlings." This was a borrowed joke from Commander Ballon.

Jhenna made a shipwide announcement. "All personnel, please prepare for atmospheric entry, descent should take roughly thirty minutes." With that, a small control stick and small touch-screen device arose from Jhenna's workstation. Normally the ships AI would take care of entry and landing, but Jhenna's reactionary and calculation abilities far exceeded that of Coeus. "Entering mesosphere in thirty seconds." She touched the control stick slightly and *Phoenix* responded, turning slightly to port and putting Varasay beneath us, out of sight from the bridge window. We would enter the atmosphere belly first, using the broad underside of *Phoenix* to slow our entry.

Soon vibrations began to shimmy the *Phoenix* as we plunged towards the surface. The ship was never designed to enter any atmosphere, but her 'flying wing' design turned out to be beneficial and the carbon-nano hull could easily withstand the rigors of atmospheric flight. Several test runs had been run on Darlon and *Phoenix* had performed remarkably.

Soon there was a noticeable slowing as we descended. "Now entering the stratosphere, engaging main engines," Jhenna announced.

"Coeus?" I asked.

"Yes Captain?"

"Bring up the foremost camera please."

The bridge window opaqued and a visual was brought up of Varasay as it rose up to meet us. Still about forty kilometers from the surface, the view was breathtaking. Small islands and Mr. Or's floating forests were clearly visible. As the main engines came online we were no longer free-falling, but flying. Spaceship turned supersonic jet in a matter of minutes.

"Now entering the troposphere, fifteen minutes to sub deployment," Jhenna updated with a calm, controlled voice. *Phoenix* shuddered slightly in the turbulence.

As I watched the view of Varasay as it flew beneath us, a swell of pride grew in my heart. If only the engineers who built *Phoenix* could see her now, screaming supersonic over the vast ocean of an alien world.

"Sir?"

Startled, I looked to my left to find Mr. Or standing next to my chair with a comm pad in his hands. "Yes Mr. Or?"

"May I speak with you?"

I saw a look of concern on his face. "Lets get the *Phoenix* landed first, then you may talk my ears off."

The four-armed science officer nodded reluctantly. "Of course," he said.

A few minutes later *Phoenix* was flying a kilometer over the voluminous, blue ocean. Touching the comm system button, I called Dr. Wesh. "Doctor, stand by for sub deployment."

"Standing by."

Jhenna slowed *Phoenix* even more and slowly brought her down to within fifty meters of the water surface. As the ship slowed, antigrav generators took over from the main engines and *Phoenix* lowered to ten meters. The water below us was crystal clear, though darkened due to *Phoenix's* shadow.

Once stationary I called to the doctor again. "Deploy when ready Mr. Wesh." The view on the screen changed from the front of the ship to the rear where two small, torpedo-shaped subs were ejected and unceremoniously fell to the water.

After several minutes, Doctor Wesh responded. "Subs deployed and operating within parameters."

"Excellent. Jhenna, put the pedal down, lets go see this island of yours." Slowly *Phoenix* rose to a safe cruising altitude and I was pulled back into my seat as the main engines reengaged.

The small volcanic islands were just a few hundred miles away and we arrived in less than half an hour. On the way there we passed over one of the floating forests. Jhenna brought us to a hover over the mass of green as Mr. Or took readings. As he analyzed the data, he announced preliminary findings. "The dominant species is a large plant that contains gas-filled bladders with which to float. They interlock tendrils of some sort to make these giant floating rafts. Other, smaller species cling to the larger plants, though it is unclear if they are symbiotic or parasitic. We should send a botanical mission back for further study, along with some entomology researchers; I'm seeing numerous forms of insect life as well. This one raft alone should keep them busy for weeks, and if there are differences between the rafts they may be here for months." After several more minutes of data gathering, we resumed course.

Jhenna deployed landing gear and guided us in slowly over an archipelago, eventually gliding in over the largest of them. Green trees and scrub dominated the crumbling edges of the isle, but the central area of the island was devoid of any life, at least that I could see. The *Phoenix* came to a hover over the vast plain of flat, black lava and off in the distance the dormant hulk of a volcano was dominant.

"Scans complete, the surface is stable," Mr. Or announced.

"Commencing with landing," Jhenna replied. "Touching down in three...two...one..." Deep booms echoed through the hull of *Phoenix* as her landing gear contacted the surface of Varasay.

Again my heart swelled with pride. "Jhenna, what do you think the engineers who built *Phoenix* would say about this?"

She thought for a moment before swiveling in her chair to

face me. "I imagine there would be quite a party involving copious amounts of liquor." I couldn't help but laugh aloud.

I then turned to my science officer. "Now Mr. Or, what has you concerned?"

"Well, Captain," he started, one hand scratching the back of his large, oval head, "during our descent something rather odd occurred to me, so I ran some scans of the ocean bottom."

"And?"

"And, well..." he trailed off. He approached me while looking down at the small comm pad in his hands. "I think this planet has been mined." At this statement, Jhenna arose and joined us.

"Mined?" she asked. "But nothing dangerous was detected during our landing scan."

"No, no, not mines of a weapon nature, mined as in strip mined, with some sort of excavators."

I contemplated this for a moment. "Well, this system has probably been here for billions of years. It's conceivable that other life forms have come here, possibly to mine for iron or other elements."

"That may be, but on this scale?" He handed me the comm pad. On it was a false-color electromagnetic image of Varasay that was taken the moment we entered orbit. The small volcanic islands could be seen, as well as faint grooves that ran latitude, presumably completely around the planet. Jhenna looked as well.

"You believe these lines represent scars from an excavator of some sort?" she asked.

Mr. Or nodded, still looking worried.

"It could just be a natural phenomenon," I suggested.

Mr. Or shook his head. "I don't think so."

"Explain."

The science officer began to pace before talking. "As you said, this system has, in all likelihood, been here for billions of years." I nodded and he continued. "Well, Varasay is highly volcanic. Billions of years of volcanism should have created some sizable land masses by now, as well as deeper oceans due to tectonic plate movement, but it's almost completely barren. Take into account the almost perfectly flat ocean bottom, and these grooves, and I can only come to one conclusion: Varasay was mined, completely stripped of her lithosphere."

Looking again at the comm pad I shook my head. "Obviously you have studied many more alien planets than I have Mr. Or, but to mine the entire lithosphere off of a planet? I don't see how the energy required to do such a thing would pay off on whatever was gained by doing so. How long ago do you think this was done?"

The officer stopped pacing. "Using current volcanism as a model, two hundred years? Maybe a little more."

"Well, if this is the case, there is still life here, so the process didn't sterilize the planet. Is there anything in the databases that would suggest who would be so advanced as to be able to do this?"

Mr. Or nodded.

"Who?"

"They're called the Parakon."

N.S. Phoenix

3

"You are familiar with Darlonian history, Captain?" asked
Mr. Or.

"I am." I said nodding. "Weren't the Parakon the ones
responsible for the flight from Shaleen by Captain Darlon?"

"That is correct. That was the last contact Darlonians had
with the Parakon, though we have had small reports of their
activity from Darlonian trading parties from other sectors."

I had studied much of the Darlonian history, even visited
the *Thunderwalker* memorial in orbit. To have been defeated as
they were, then to start from scratch on an alien world was a
testament to Captain Darlon and the tenacity of the Shaleen
people.

I looked at the pad in my hand once more before returning
it to Mr. Or. "Do we know why they do this?"

"Some reports that have trickled through say they are at

war with a race called the Staelons. Other reports say they fight over a blue hyper-dwarf star, a source of unlimited power. I can only assume they do this to a planet for raw materials, too build more ships, but that's just speculation."

Crossing my arms, I absently tapped my chin with my forefinger. Eventually I nodded. "Thank you Mr. Or, please gather whatever information you can. We'll file a special report with DSEA upon our return. Coeus?"

"Yes, Captain?"

"We're you listening in?"

"Of course."

"If what Mr. Or presumes is true, it happened a long time ago, but please activate all long-range scanners and sensors. Tap into our two new satellites if you need to. No sense in not playing it safe."

"Very well."

I touched a comm button on the arm of my chair. "Exploratory team, depart whenever you are ready. Please stay alert. You have two hours."

The time went by uneventfully, even I donned a suit and departed the ship for half an hour. I watched as survey crews took samples of rock, lichen and some small clumps of mossy looking plants. One crew member even found what looked like a small lizard. The crew named him Poppel, then he was humanely sacrificed for science.

Small fissures had formed in the lava over the centuries and harbored small pools of water. Water samples were taken in hopes of finding bacteria or other microbial life.

I walked a distance away and looked out over the lava plain and the ocean beyond. I could have easily convinced myself that I was somewhere in Hawaii, minus the spacesuit of course. Some crew had taken ground gliders back to the edge of the island to take samples of the trees and plants there. Other gliders went out over the water in hopes of catching some sea life for study. I could almost convince myself they were just tourists out for a walk.

And in retrospect, that wasn't far from the truth.

Turning back, I looked at *Phoenix* as she squatted on her four enormous landing gear legs. Her four hydrogen-compress engines were also visible, capable of thermonuclear fusion and extreme power and speed when needed; most notably when breaking free of planetary gravity. The neat thing about these engines is that they did not dump radiation, it was safely collected for later disposal. Her old Helium-3 powered engines were not so kind.

As compared to a lot of the ships in the DSEA, *Phoenix* was a rather small ship, but seeing her like this, squatting on a huge plane of blackened lava, she looked enormous and, well, pretty darned awesome sitting there. I was proud to be her captain, be she regarded as small or not.

Eventually all crew members returned to the ship. Our plans were to visit at least three islands, perhaps more if life were found, and it was. Now a question was to see what genetic diversity there was between the islands. As light was fading at our current location, it was decided to chase the sun in order to have plenty of light at our next stop.

I had no sooner returned to the bridge and taken my chair when Mr. Or said aloud, "We may have company sir. A small ship to our east, bearing down quickly."

I hurriedly accompanied Mr. Or's station. He had the ship magnified on the HoloTable. The main body of the ship was a vertical disk. Two sets of wing protruded from the sides and were mounted with engines, as well as what looked like weapons, cannons of some sort.

"How did we not see them when we entered the system?" I asked.

"They must have been on the other side of the planet. Coeus just patched this information through to my station, one of our satellites just picked it up."

"Open a hail to them, all languages," I requested.

Mr. Or touched the hologram keyboard. "Go ahead."

"Unidentified approaching ship, we are here on a mission

of exploration only, please respond." After thirty seconds of no response, and no change in their course and speed, I decided to take the offensive. Quickly returning to my chair, I made a ship-wide announcement. "All stations lockdown. We have incoming visitors. Intentions unknown." I then turned to Jhenna. "Lets go aquatic. One kilometer off the south side of the island." She nodded and the ship filled with the humming of main and hover engines coming online. "Coeus, leave landing gear down."

"Very well," came his reply.

*Phoenix* lifted off quickly but remained only a dozen meters in elevation. Jhenna punched the main engines and *Phoenix* turned a one-eighty and surged south. Within seconds we were over the ocean and quickly to our coordinates. Then *Phoenix* took an abrupt nose dive into the clear water.

"Let's take her all the way down Jhenna. Coeus, engage cloaking field." The cloaking field would basically camouflage us by imaging the bottom under the ship and reflecting it upwards. It would also hide us from sensor sweeps.

Jhenna glided us to the bottom quickly and landed us on the bedrock, then shut down engines. The ocean bottom was visible on the viewscreen, but there was not much to see; some sand bars, a couple of small fish-like creatures, a few rocks but no coral or other forms of life. This was only the third time *Phoenix* had gone aquatic, the first two were just training exercises. She wasn't very graceful underwater, but gracefulness wasn't needed.

I joined Mr. Or's station again and Jhenna followed. "The ship has slowed considerably, Captain. I think our sudden disappearance has confused them." Indeed the ship had slowed and lowered in elevation, it seemed to have assumed a defensive posture. Mr. Or zoomed out so both the ship and our quickly departed island were in view. Our visitors then turned south and made a large loop in order to come upon the island from a different angle. It looked as if they would pass directly over us.

"I am picking up power surges on the ship," Mr. Or said.

"I would assume they are charging weapons," Jhenna speculated. Sure enough, the cannon-like pods on the wings began to glow blue.

"Does the ship configuration match anything in the Darlonian database?" I asked.

Mr. Or shook his head in the negative.

Returning to my seat I made several quick commands. "Mr. Wesh, charge all HyPhos cannons and bring pulse-lasers online, pre-focus them precisely two hundred meters forward.

"Jhenna, ready engines at full thrust. When that ship passes over solid ground I want to come out of the water at the very edge of the island and up behind them. Let's assume the element of surprise.

"Mr. Or, ready communications, all languages, all

50

frequencies.

"Coeus, as soon as the ship moves retract landing gear, we don't need their resistance in the water. Also, as soon as we leave the water, disengage cloaking field and engage forward hull shields. Let's assume hostility on their part until otherwise proven."

"Ship continues to slow, but still on approach, they should pass over us in a matter of minutes," the science officer explained.

It was probably the longest four minutes of my life. I was probably being overly aggressive in confronting this ship, but I was taking no chances. We were thirty seven light years from home and our jump ring was up in orbit. It was Darlon policy to send rescue missions if a ship failed to return from a mission within a reasonable amount of time, but damned if I was going to have to be rescued on my maiden foray. Or worse yet, the crew killed and the *Phoenix* destroyed.

Mr. Or spoke up, "ship is passing overhead now, just to our starboard side."

Nodding I touched the shipwide comm button. "Hold tight everyone, this may get bumpy." Mr. Or held onto the HoloTable with all four arms. I gripped my armrests.

"Ship is now over land."

I smiled. "Floor it Jhenna."

The sudden surge forward was alarming as *Phoenix* shot forward. Jhenna guided the ship with extreme accuracy as we followed the underwater rise of the island upwards. Suddenly the ship was almost vertical and *Phoenix* exploded from the surface of the ocean.

Jhenna quickly brought the ship back horizontal as we shot across open land. The entire procedure took less than ten seconds and we now braked to a hover behind the other ship.

It was huge, much bigger than I expected by looking at it in the hologram. It was easily twice the size of *Phoenix*. "Forward shields are up, Captain," Coeus explained.

"All weapons locked," Mr. Wesh reported.

"Communications open," Mr. Or said.

Both ships had come to a complete stop, the visiting ship made no move to turn or flee. "Greetings, I am Captain Dankin of the Starship *Phoenix*. To what do we owe the pleasure of your visit?" Several minutes elapsed before a reply came.

"They are requesting visual, Captain," said Mr. Or. I nodded and the viewscreen flickered from an exterior view to an interior view of the other ship.

"I am Captain Narell of the *R.S. Heraway*. That was an – interesting maneuver Captain, you have us at a disadvantage." The Captain, looking more less human, was a massive man, standing at least eight feet tall. His broad shoulders and thick arms strained at his uniform of orange and gold. Deep-set, dark green eyes and a strong, pronounced jawline gave him a menacing quality that was quite, I must admit, intimidating.

"My apologies for coming to the party with guns drawn Captain Narell, but we are a long way from home and in unfamiliar space." I stood from my chair and walked closer to the viewscreen. "And it was you coming towards us with weapons powered up."

The Captain stood quiet and stoically for a moment, his green eyes piercing. "Who are you and why are you here Captain Dankin?"

Lacing my hands behind my back, I smiled. "We are Darlonians, and we are here on an exploratory mission, as my first communique explained. Our long range scans found this planet and we are here to learn about it and the system. Nothing more. Now, I believe a reciprocation would be in order here."

The Captain smiled in return, his teeth were like perfectly square chunks of black marble. "We are Staelons, and we are here to inspect the recovery progress of this planet."

Thinking quickly of Mr. Or's information, I replied, "I've heard of your race, apparently you are at war with a people called the Parakon."

The Captain's smile vanished in a blink. His green eyes pierced me to the core. "Oh yes, Captain. Yes we are. And have been for over six hundred years."

I was quiet for a moment. "The Parakon destroyed a planet called Shaleen over twelve hundred years ago," I explained. "The planet I come from holds distant ancestors of those who survived."

Suddenly Captain Narell's posture and eyes softened. "I believe, Captain Dankin, that we are on the same side here," he said and turned to his right. "Tal-et-Or, stand down all weapons."

I turned to Mr. Or for verification. He nodded. "Mr. Wesh, please disengage and power down all weapons," I called out, then turned back to the viewscreen. "We're wasting a lot of power hovering here like this Captain, and the sun is setting. May I suggest traveling to a sunnier area of the planet to land and talk?"

Captain Narell nodded. "Lead the way, Captain."

We cut communication and I addressed Jhenna. "Find us a spot further west, a place where both ships can land. Proceed when ready."

"Yes, Captain, and might I say, that was very well done."

"Learning surprise-diplomacy is mandatory when you have four brothers Jhenna, especially when all four were older than you."

I returned to my chair and sat down with a sigh of relief. I was never one for confrontation, much less with an alien species on a lost world dozens of light years from home, but I think I pulled it off pretty well.

The *Phoenix* and *Heraway* flew side by side for several thousands kilometers. Eventually we arrived at another volcanic island similar to the one we'd left; a dominant, but dormant volcano at one end and many kilometers of flat, hardened lava at the other. We slowed slightly and let the *Heraway* proceed and land first. What I thought were trailing spars from the *Heraways* wings were actually landing gear. As the *Heraway* descended, the wings rotated downward and the ship lowered and settled on the cracked, black lava.

Jhenna brought the *Phoenix* down a hundred meters away before reestablishing contact with *Heraway*. When visual was up on the viewscreen, the captain had two crew members standing next to him.

"Captain, this is my sub-commander, Lieutenant Brath, and my science officer, Lieutenant Novas," Narell explained and I introduced my bridge crew in return. "Officer Orthalidotian, you are Ketarian, correct?" the Staelon captain asked.

"Why, yes, I am," Or replied, a bit surprised.

"I met a Ketarian ship's captain many, many years ago at a trading post in the Baston sector. Name was Hereshemorell. You're people are – quite fond of long names. Anyway, he was a noble man, we got on well."

"I am unfamiliar with that House name, but then again I

have not been back to Ketaria in many decades."

After several more minutes of pleasantries, Narell brought the subject back around. "I am old, Captain, at least by our people's standards. I and everyone aboard this ship have been put out to pasture, so to speak. Instead of commanding a warship, I am now commanding a research vessel." The captain's two crew officers had returned to their stations, it was just he and I talking now.

"I can't say I disagree," he continued. "As we get older our minds slow and decision-making begins to falter. Not a good combination for a warship commander. But I served my time and was released from command with honors. Though it still pains me to get up in the morning knowing I will study planets instead of enemy tactics.

"You see Captain, the war we are engaged in used to be about a  blue hyper-dwarf star called Kaepec 428, but has instead become a war to stop the carnage the Parakon dole out on planets and civilizations. It became clear that the war did not justify the carnage, that our fight over a star was not worth the death and destruction. So we pulled back, we pulled out of the war. But the destruction by the Parakon continued. They continued to rake planets of their resources and build their armadas of warships, building their empire to protect against anyone who would try and claim Kaepec."

The captain looked down for a few moments before continuing. "So our people decided to reengage the Parakon, but not to fight over Kaepec, but to stop the destruction they reaped wherever they went. Entire civilizations obliterated for the sake of strengthening their mindless waring mentality. The death and destruction they have caused is beyond understanding.

"So we have engaged the Parakon now for over six hundred years. It is all we know. It is all we live for. And those planets that do fall to the Parakon, we try to repair the damage. We reseed the planets with life in hopes they will flourish again one day.

"And we are here to check on a planet that was destroyed by the Parakon almost three hundred years ago. Sometimes the reseeding does not work, but in this case, it is working as planned."

I thought deeply on the Captains' words when he was finished. I had learned so much over the last few months, but the knowledge that I had come from a race of people ignorant of the vast diversity of life in the cosmos was the hardest to fully comprehend and digest. And here I was, on an alien world, talking to an alien race about a six hundred year old war with yet another alien race. It was almost too much to comprehend.

"I feel your plight Captain," I said to the viewscreen. "I come from a race of people who seemed almost too happy to fight and engage war. The need was so great that they eventually destroyed themselves and poisoned my home world." I thought carefully before speaking again. "While I would like to offer help in your mission, I have a council I must answer to first. Otherwise I would offer whatever help I could."

Captain Narell bowed. "Your offer of assistance is honorable Captain, but we rarely accept assistance. It is not our wish to pull another race into an endless war."

"Be that as it may Captain, Darlon has significant defenses at its disposal and , as you can imagine, perhaps a special interest in joining you against the Parakon. I promise that I will bring this matter to my commanders when we return. Your mission is one of reverence and in keeping with peace, how can I turn my back on what you stand for?"

The Staelon captain stood quietly for a moment, seeming to reflect on his past and present. "You honor me with your words Captain. Though I --"

"Captain," came a voice on the Staelon bridge.

Captain Narell looked off to the side with no small amount of irritability. "What is it flight officer?"

"Incoming Parakon scout ship. Mark two four nine mark one four."

"ETA?"

"Approximately fifteen minutes, Captain."

Narell looked back up at the viewscreen. "Captain, even their scout ships are war-faring. I suggest you leave now, they will not come peacefully, the *Heraway* will distract them. "

"You don't seem surprised by their presence," I commented as Jhenna powered up engines.

"We suspected they shadowed us on our voyage here. They're just keeping an eye on us. They will not directly take on the *Heraway*, nor us them. We both know we would only obliterate each other."

"Didn't you say they will not come peacefully?" I asked.

The *Heraway* Captain smiled. "I meant for you, Captain. They know who we are, but they seem to be interested in *Phoenix*," he finished, but then added, "It was a pleasure meeting you Captain, I hope our paths cross again one day."

"Likewise," I replied and communications were severed. By now Jhenna had *Phoenix* powered up and lifting off. Once landing gear was up, the ship surged out over the ocean and, as we reached target speed, Jhenna pulled back on her control stick and *Phoenix* shot for the sky.

"I have the Parakon ship Captain," Mr. Or announced. I moved to the hologram station where the Parakon vessel was now hovering. My first impression was that the ship looked like a scythe with a very short handle. The engines were located on the back side of the 'handle' and the ship flew point forward. Very menacing indeed.

I called over my shoulder, "Jhenna, ETA to the jump ring?"

"Approximately ten minutes."

"*Heraway* moving to intercept," said Mr. Or. We watched as the Staelon ship rose quickly through the atmosphere, its leading edge beginning to glow from atmospheric friction. The two ships were more or less heading directly towards one another, but suddenly the Parakon ship changed course. As it did so it launched a salvo of what looked like hundreds of small missiles in the direction of the *Heraway*. They streaked across the blue sky leaving small contrails in their wake.

Mr. Or further announced, "Parakon ship has changed course sir. They are on an intercept course."

"Jhenna," I said. "Lets make that ten minutes five instead." She nodded and pushed the engines to maximum safe thrust, quickly reaching mach eighteen, the atmospheric limit to what *Phoenix* could handle.

"The *Heraway* has been hit, sir," Officer Or proclaimed. "Their forward shields took out most of the detonations, but one damaged a port wing. I believe they are trying to make an emergency landing."

Nodding, I looked back to Jhenna, "ETA?"

"Four and a half minutes."

"Can we reengage the jump ring before the Parakon reach us?"

After a moment of calculations, Jhenna responded. "By thirty three point six seconds."

I walked to the HoloStation and watched the Parakon ship pursue us. Cones of white fire emitted from its engines as it shrieked through the upper atmosphere. "Jhenna, calculate how much harder we can push the engines as the atmosphere becomes less dense and make it happen."

"Yes, Captain. Once the jump ring is reengaged, what should be our coordinates?"

"Anywhere but here –," I broke off, an idea suddenly breaking surface of my conscious. I thought deeply for a moment, then went to Jhenna's station. I put one hand on the back of her chair, the other on the armrest. "Question, is it possible to fire a weapon through the jump membrane?"

She looked perplexed. "Curious. I do not know. To my knowledge it has never been done."

"Listen, we relock the jump ring and set coordinates directly behind the Parakon ship. We open the jump membrane and fire HyPhos rounds. It will take them from behind. Will it work?"

Jhenna thought for a moment. "I see no reason why it shouldn't."

"Let's do it. Coeus, start remote power-up of the jump ring. Also, engage jump ring thrusters, I want it moving as fast as possible on intercept. It should gain us a few more seconds."

"Yes, Captain."

Over the next few minutes Jhenna increased speed as we left the atmosphere and soon the jump ring was within view.

"Standby mag-locks Coeus," Jhenna called out. We had to slow considerably for docking, but still we were moving at over a thousand kilometers an hour.

"Captain! The Parakon have fired on us. ETA in ninety seconds!" cried Mr. Or.

"Mr. Wesh!" I called out, "charge all aft pulse lasers, standby auto-guidance!"

"They'll be ready, sir!" came the reply.

I walked to Mr. Or's station. "Jhenna, as soon as mag-locks are engaged, calculate speed and trajectory of the Parakon ship and proceed at opening the jump membrane. Fire all HyPhos cannons simultaneously. Once the rounds are through the membrane, terminate power to the jump ring, I don't want any wreckage coming back through and hitting us."

I watched the holographic images of hundreds of Parakon rounds bearing down on *Phoenix*. "Immediately after termination of jump ring, raise rear shields Mr. Wesh and fire at will."

"Yes, sir!"

Jhenna quickly closed the space between ship and ring. As soon as *Phoenix* was in position, mag locks gripped the ring and Jhenna initiated power up.

"Twenty seconds!" said Mr. Or. He brought up dual holograms, one of the *Phoenix*, the other of the Parakon ship. Blue fire swirled and shot forward from the jump ring to a precise point ahead of us, then opened. The Phoenix bucked at the discharge of all five HyPhos cannons and five balls of white fire shot forth. Switching views, we watched a shimmering black disc suddenly form behind the Parakon ship. Suddenly five balls of fire erupted from the membrane and impacted the stern of the Parakon ship, a direct hit on the engines.

"Ten seconds!"

"Now Mr. Wesh!"

The jump ring terminated and hundreds of pulse lasers went to work. In a matter of seconds hundreds of explosions erupted, lighting up space behind *Phoenix*. Despite the lasers, a few Parakon rounds made it through the defense, but harmlessly exploded against the rear shielding.

Moments later, it was over. Mr. Or and I watched the Parakon ship slowly begin to spin end over end as explosions rocked the main body of the ship. The engine section had been completely destroyed and a wide, firey field of wreckage and debris surrounded the vessel.

With my heart still racing, I returned to my chair and sat quietly for a few minutes. This definitely was not what I was expecting on our first exploratory mission. Once my heart rate dropped to a more sane level, I turned in my chair. "Mr. Or, status of the *Heraway*?"

He waved in the air and brought up a new visual. "They landed safely, but their ship is badly damaged."

"Open a link please." In moments Captain Narell appeared on the viewscreen. "Captain, it seems our paths, as you wished, have crossed again. Do you require assistance?" I inquired.

The captain, looking none the worse for wear, responded with what must have been reluctance. "Thank you for the offer Captain, but we can manage repairs. I am sorry we could not have been more helpful, the Parakon do not usually engage reconnaissance ships. We were caught off-guard."

"Well, as you said, they took a sudden interest in *Phoenix*, I guess they were willing to go to extremes to learn about us."

"Yes, that may be," he said, then stood straight and squared his shoulders. "We monitored your actions from here and once again – your maneuvers surprised me. I don't understand your weapon, but it worked."

I laughed aloud. "Trust me Captain, those maneuvers surprised us as well, they were pretty much made it up as we went along. And that 'weapon' isn't a weapon at all, it's our way of travel."

"Be that as it may, for having never encountered a Parakon ship, you handled yourselves remarkably."

"Coming from an honored, retired warship commander, I'll take that as a gracious compliment," I said with a smile.

We talked for a while longer about the Parakon and the *Heraway* sent us an information packet concerning all they new about their enemy. I thanked him profusely and informed him I would pass the information on to the DSEA.

Captain Narell nodded, then seemed to think for a moment. "Captain, this planet you're from, this – Darlon – of yours, is it a mixed-species world?"

I nodded. "Darlon currently plays host to over thirty-two different peoples from our sector of space and beyond. It's quite a diverse world. Why do you ask?"

He seemed to choose his words carefully before answering. "As I said earlier Captain, I am getting old, and judging by our current situation, a situation I am responsible for, perhaps it is time I consider another line of work, one that does not involve a ship. I wonder if your Darlonian government would welcome a Staelon Ambassador?"

At this statement, the Sub Commander of the *Heraway* spoke up. "Captain, I –," he started, but Harell raised his hand and turned to address his subordinate. "Mr. Brath," he started, then

65

sighed before continuing, "what just happened to *Heraway* should never have happened, *wouldn't* have happened in my younger years. To almost be destroyed by a Parakon scout ship? My legacy would have crumbled and my honor tarnished. Perhaps it is time I step down and accept that I am a young theletorn no more."

Audio had no translation for what a theletorn was, but I could sense, even over a comm link, how difficult this was for the Captain. His voice wavered between anger, frustration and hint of sad revelation. All five crew members on the *Heraway* bridge now faced the captain, all with looks of surprise.

"Part of the *Heraway's* mission, albeit a small part, also includes meeting and exploring new civilizations, correct?" The Sub Commander nodded, but did not speak. "And it is true that we have Staelon representatives on other planets as well, yes?" Another nod. "So perhaps this is a sign, perhaps there is a reason for meeting these people from Darlon," he said and paused before continuing. "And besides, all my life has been about war and now, perhaps, I'd like a little peace; to live out the rest of my days learning about other people and cultures instead of studying war, planets, rocks and dust," he finished. Though his voice was pained, his body posture still projected strength and pride.

Sub Commander Brath looked at his captain for a long time, then approached him. He held up a clinched fist and placed it on his his commander's chest, and Narell returned the gesture. "To have served with you for most of my career has been an honor Captain and – I understand your wishes. But what will I tell Command?"

Narell turned back to me. "Thoughts, Captain?"

"You would be welcomed Captain Narell," I said with a nod. "Especially with your knowledge of the Parakon."

"Tell them," Narell said, turning back to his sub commander, "that I have gone on a recruiting mission. You saw what their technology did to that Parakon ship – Captain Brath."

Brath started to speak, then stopped with a slightly stunned look on his face.

"I have a small transport ship Captain Dankin, I will arrive at your ship within two hours. Right now I have some promotions to dictate and oaths to record."

Communications were severed and I returned to my seat. Again I sat quietly for a few minutes, but not thinking on the last fifteen minutes, but rather how proud I was of my crew. The *Phoenix* was not a warship and the crew was not trained in aspects of extreme combat, but still, we kept our wits when confronted with a threat. I touched a comm button. "Mr. Wesh?"

After a pause, "Yes, Captain?"

"Well done."

A pause. "Thank you, Captain."

"Jhenna? Mr. Or?" they both turned towards me, "well done, and Jhenna, that was some amazing piloting."

Mr. Or, looking a bit flustered, replied, "Thank you Captain. In all my years aboard *Classtoria*, nothing like this has ever happened. This was – stimulating to be sure."

Jhenna smiled, nodded and turned back to her station. I pulled up a small monitor from my armrest and read some reports. We held station in awaiting the arrival of Captain Narell, so I figured I'd review some data. There were no injuries due to the few rounds that impacted our shields from the Parakon ship, but the rear shielding itself did suffer some loss in power. Nothing that couldn't be fixed, but still, they should have held at full power. I made a note in the system to have Lieutenant Laylop have a look when we returned to the Hyperion System.

Our encounter with the Parakon ship was also documented, and that took a full hour. It seems no matter where you go in space, there's always paperwork to do.

At least I didn't have to sit at a desk.

4

Captain Narell arrived aboard *Phoenix* without incident. If I thought he was an imposing figure on a viewscreen, he was even more so in person. Easily two foot taller than I, my neck quickly became fatigued looking up at him.

Before departing the bridge to meet him in the hanger deck, I'd left orders for Jhenna to proceed first to Herra, then Vista to deploy the final two satellites. After some pleasantries once he came aboard, I invited him to the commissary for a glass of trill, an artisanal, mildly alcoholic drink prized on Darlon. We now sat in plush chairs across a table from one another.

"This is divine Captain," he said, taking a sip. "What is it called again?"

"It's called trill, made from fermented fruits. The process is somewhat of an art form, or so I've heard. And please, call me Terry."

He nodded. "I am Ghesh, and thank you again, Terry, for your hospitality." The captain had shed his uniform before leaving *Heraway*, now he wore a floor-length robe with a wide belt around his waist. The robe was deep green and decorated with white pin striping.

"You're welcome. Darlon is a rich, diverse culture, you will be welcomed there." I leaned back in my chair and took another sip of trill. "I must say, that was an on the spot decision, to leave the *Heraway* I mean."

Ghesh shook his head and looked at me with his bright green eyes. His voice was deep in the quiet room. "Not as much as you may think. I have been debating for some time of leaving command. There comes a point, I believe, where sometimes the mind grows weary, even from that which you used to cherish." He paused to reflect for a moment before continuing. "My two sons are well grown now and have their own commands in the Staelon Fleet. My mate, Dren, passed away some years ago as well, right about the time I was retired. I accepted the position aboard *Heraway* to keep myself occupied and it worked for a while, but I now feel the need to start anew, challenge myself in other ways."

Nodding, I said, "I can certainly understand the need to start anew; and sorry for your loss."

Ghesh met my eyes. "Thank you, Terry. Dren was a good mate, and fine mother." He took another sip of his drink. "So, tell me how you became part of the Darlon culture."

The abbreviated story I told him covered the main points, starting with the signal received from Dione to being rescued by the *Classtoria*. When I was finished, Ghesh's expression had turned to, as best I could tell, one of slight horror.

"That is – quite a story. That you survived at all is beyond comprehension."

We finished our drinks and I rose to refill our glasses. "So," I said, returning with full glasses, "tell me more about the Parakon. How is it they can strip a planet like they did in this system?"

He sipped his drink before answering. "My, this is delicious. Reminds me of a drink back in the fleet called prelon; fermented blood of the chall fish," he said, then paused to gather his thoughts, then leaned his immense frame back into his chair. "I am not a scientist, Terry, I am a warship commander, albeit retired, so please forgive me my lack of the scientific aspect." I nodded and he continued. "The Parakon and Staclons, among other races, used to war over Kaepec 428, a blue hyper-dwarf star. It is the only one known to exist and is very small and very dense. How it has not become a micro black hole is not within the realms of my understanding.

"It was discovered over a millennium ago by a peaceful people called the Qwentis and, somehow, someone discovered

71

how to harvest tiny bits of it, amounts so small it was barely visible to the naked eye. Even this small amount was powerful enough to supply massive amounts of energy, primarily for ships engines.

"At first, the Quentis shared their knowledge with other species, but as word spread of this remarkable form of energy, the demand became too high. Their plight literally started in just trying to defend themselves from the sudden greed they were faced with. Then the Parakon moved in with force so extreme and violent that the Quintis were completely annihilated.

"My distant ancestors teamed up with other species to try and take the sector that holds the star from the Parakon. They wared for over a hundred years, then an event opened their eyes to the devastation they brought upon world after world."

"What was that?" I asked.

"They took Staelon, our homeworld. Until then it was only rumored as to what they did to these planets, but then they saw first-hand –," he trailed off. "Millions were killed, the ecosystem totally obliterated. The Staelons brought every warship they could muster in an attempt to stop them, but ultimately they were unsuccessful. They were able to to rescue tens of thousands of people, as well as knowledge-bases and other items before they were destroyed." His eyes focused on nothingness over my shoulder.

"In the face of this devastation, they quickly pulled out of the war in order to flee and come to terms with what they had witnessed. Without a homeworld, they became completely spacefaring.

"Over a decade went by as they rebuilt what was left of our people. Eventually it was decided to reengage the Parakon. My ancestors knew they could not stop them, and did not try. So they developed tactics that greatly hindered their ability to strengthen their war machine. They built more ships, stronger ships, bigger ships and when they were ready, well, the Parakon had never witnessed such a devastating attack on them those first few days.

"And then they vanished, leaving the Parakon in a state of disarray. They were far from defeated, mind you, but they were left questioning their might for the first time since taking Kaepec. Since then we've become a constant worry to them, constantly gnashing at their heels. They have not stopped their war machine, but we have slowed them," he finished with another sip of trill.

We sat quietly for a while, each of us lost in our own thoughts.

Eventually, I asked, "How do they do it?"

"Rake a planet? Like I said, I'm no scientist, but if I remember correctly the term for their machine is called an antigrav laser. Or something to that effect. These machines are placed in orbit and massive lasers cut into the lithosphere. They cut to a certain depth, then transport the material into orbit where it is sorted somehow. Water is left behind and unusable material is ejected into space. They seek iron, carbon; anything that can be used to build ships and make weapons. The process can take up to several months, depending on the size of the planet."

Ghesh and I sat quietly for a while. My mind could not quite wrap around what Ghesh was telling me. Billions of years of evolution, destroyed in a matter of weeks. And they had been doing this for over a millennia? How many thousands of worlds had been eliminated? How many millions of ships had been built?

Suddenly, something wasn't sitting well in my mind. Some part of the puzzle wasn't shaped quite right, wasn't fitting where it should. "There's got to be more to this story," I said eventually.

Ghesh looked puzzled. "What do you mean?"

During my recent schooling, I found that, when stuck on a problem, getting up and pacing helped sort things out, so I stood and started walking back and forth across the commissary floor. "After a thousand years you would think the Parakon would have harvested enough of this star to suit their needs for thousands of more years. Why do they continue to defend it so violently, and with such overwhelming force?"

Ghesh nodded. "I have often asked those questions myself, but have yet to find an answer, not that I dwell on them overly, I had Parakon to chase down and destroy."

Shaking my head, I said, "Something else is going on Ghesh. I just doesn't make sense to spend so much time and expend so much energy. To render basically lifeless so many worlds and sacrifice so many lives on both sides, just for little pieces of a star. They could have harvested all they needed for endless generations, then departed for places unknown and let others fight over Kaepec. So why are they still doing it?"

Ghesh placed a now empty glass on the table with care, then leaned back into his chair again. With his giant left hand he rubbed his shallow beard in contemplation. "Perhaps, Terry, it's simply about power and domination. You mentioned your species seemed to go out of their way to war with one another. Surely your history is laced with dictators trying to rule all."

I could only nod at this statement. "Too many of them, and I will concede your line of thinking, but still, something feels odd about this."

"Indeed. I will relay a message back to our commanders through *Heraway*. Perhaps they can take a closer look at what's going on around Kaepec with fresh eyes. Do you have a communications station I could use?"

We departed the commissary for the bridge. Upon arrival Jhenna announced, "Satellites at Herra and Vista have been deployed. Awaiting your orders."

I took my Captain's chair, leaned back and looked out the bridge window at the glowing gas giant that was Vista. Its outer atmosphere was resplendent in multicolor bands of stormy turbulence and soft rings of dust and gasses encircled the equator, extending out tens of thousands of kilometers. It was indeed a beautiful world. Gesh approached and stood by my side, looking out at the splendor as well. "There have been many times in my career that I have gazed upon the beauty of our cosmos and wondered why war rages so pandemic. It seems such a waste."

Nodding my acquiescence, I said, "I feel that way as well, and this is still all so new to me, I can only imagine the depth of your experiences."

We watched the ethereal beauty for a moment longer, even Jhenna and Mr. Or seemed transfixed. Eventually I pulled myself back to reality. "While this mission was supposed to last several days, I think it prudent, under recent circumstances, to call it a day and head back to Darlon. Set a course Jhenna. Let's go home."

As the jump ring powered up, we opened a communication to the *Heraway* and the now retired Captain Narell relayed concerns and questions of our discussion to Brath. The newly minted Captain nodded. "Those are legitimate questions, I will pass them along upon our return to Fleet. May you find peace in your journeys Captain Narell, and you as well

Captain Dankin."

"Thank you Captain, I'm sure we'll meet again, I wish you safe travels as well," I replied.

After communications were severed, Jhenna announced, "Ready for primary jump, Captain."

"Proceed, and you have the bridge Jhenna," I said, then turned to Ghesh. "What is your opinion on getting your hands dirty with grease and tinkering with tools?"

Ghesh smiled and raised his massive hands. "Lead the way," he said.

4

I wish I could say our trip home was uneventful, but it
turned out to be far from the peaceful trip we'd enjoyed out to
Varasay.

The first day, however, *was* uneventful as Ghesh and I got
to know one another. After a good nights sleep, we met in the
commissary for a breakfast. I'd arrived first and ordered eggs,
bacon and toast with a Darlonian beverage similar to coffee.
When Ghesh arrived he looked down at my plate. I offered him a
spare fork and he tried the eggs, then tentatively accepted a strip
of bacon. "Eggs I am familiar with, they are popular in Fleet
cafeterias; bird, fish and reptile. But this – bacon, as you call it –
is delicious!" he said with a thundering voice. I could only smile
in return.

"Order what you wish from Chef Boonod, he'll prepare

however much you wish."

The eight foot Ghesh turned and approached the short, skinny man who stood in his circular cooking station. The physique difference between the two of them was startling. "I will have – fifteen eggs and – twenty pieces of the bacon strips."

Boonod's eyes widened, but then asked, "How, Captain, may I prepare said eggs for your dining pleasure?"

Ghesh turned to me with a question in his eyes. "Um, he'll take them sunny-side up, please Chef," I replied.

"Very well, will there be a beverage with this morning's meal? We have howen, which is a fruit juice or what Captain Dankin is having, qwen. Its quite energizing."

"Yes, I'm sure it is, but I believe I will have a liter of triff," he replied, then looked at me. "It was quite delicious."

Boonod's eyes and my smile grew even wider. "What?" Ghesh asked, suddenly looking concerned. "Is that an inappropriate beverage to order? I didn't offend anyone, did I?"

I laughed, "No, not at all. Triff is alcoholic and – well – not many people drink alcohol with a morning meal."

"Oh, I see," he said, and seemed to think carefully for a moment. "In light of my retirement," he said steadfastly, "I believe a liter of triff is called for, be it for a morning meal or evening."

I looked at him for a moment, then said with a smile, "I

suppose you've earned the right, Captain."

After our morning meal, which the Captain devoured with relish, I escorted Ghesh on a tour of the *Phoenix*, stopping at the memorial to my two long-ago friends. After explaining who they were, Ghesh had a sad, soft look to his powerful, angular face. "I have lost many under my command, Terry. It is a burden we must bear. It is a requirement of our chair and position. I share your feelings of loss."

We continued the tour, ending up in the main hanger deck where my custom zephyr still sat in its cradle. "*Phoenix* is a remarkable ship, Terry, especially one that can go from the vacuum of space, to atmospheric flight to a submersible."

Nodding, I replied, "I have the engineers on Darlon to thank for all of that, they're remarkable ship-builders." I then showed him my zephyr and explained the modifications I was making.

"We have a similar transport," Ghesh explained, "the one I arrived in yesterday. They are called *arets* and are used to travel between ships. Very valuable, especially in large armadas."

After explaining my problems with the steering modulators, Ghesh thought for a moment. "Perhaps the problem is not a mechanical one. Perhaps it's in the programming?" he replied with a quizzical crook in his brow.

"I –," started, but then stopped with my mouth open in

wonder, a greasy modulator in my hand. Why hadn't I thought of that? Smiling I said, "That is the only logical explanation."

We talked at length of the Staelon Fleet, Darlon and other things in general as we reconfigured the zephyr software and reassembled the main drives for the antigrav pads. We sat at a steel worktable across from one another, and it was apparent Ghesh was no stranger to rolling up his sleeves and getting a little dirty. When I commented on it, he said, "When one's ship is damaged in battle, it behooves one to know how to fix things, and very quickly I might add. The alternative is have one's pashtak blown to smithereens." I didn't ask, as I could very well guess what a pashtak was.

He also told me about other races of people involved with the Staelon effort to stop the Parakon; the Yehwish, the Perishmon, the Sherepen. Together they'd formed the Staelon Alliance. The Alliance had no central homeworld or outpost, thus keeping the Parakon guessing as to where the Alliance armada was stationed or hiding out.

Many effective attack maneuvers were implemented by the Alliance, but in centuries of fighting, the best technique in slowing the Parakon were surprise attacks at almost the speed of light. A Parakon sector was chosen at random, then up to five allied vessels would shriek through the system, picking off as many Parakon vessels as possible with phase cannons. These attacks were highly effective at not only destroying many ships, but also demoralizing crews of those that were not.

"Why attack at such high speeds?" I inquired.

Ghesh smiled wickedly. "When you approach that fast, their sensor sweeps are useless. They may only achieve a five to ten second warning. Not enough to defend themselves."

Eventually the conversation turned to Darlon and the fact there had never been a war in their twelve hundred year history. Ghesh took interest after I described my home by the sea. "I – cannot imagine such a peaceful existence. I have visited many beautiful worlds, but to call one my home will be vastly different than the life I've known."

"Well, after we get you registered with DSEA, you will be assigned a home of your own. You can choose anywhere on the planet, or on one of hundreds of orbiting stations if you so choose."

"Assigned?"

"Yes," I said, selecting a small laser welder with which to repair a copper coil. "No one owns land on Darlon, the planet belongs to everyone. You will be assigned a home wherever you wish and you may stay in it as long as you like. You may also move to another location if you so choose as well," I said and, finishing the micro-weld, inspected my work.

"And how does one go about paying for such a home – or

other necessities?" Ghesh asked as he began disassembling one of the four balancing modulators from the zephyr. "I only know one thing in life Terry, War and combat. I do not know what I can offer in order to earn my way in this new life."

I thought on his question for a moment. "I would suggest being a teacher."

An incredulous look came across his face. "A teacher?" he scoffed. "What could I possibly teach?"

I shrugged while inserting the coil back into its housing. "You've been all over the galaxy and visited many worlds. You could teach a class on cultures or planetary governments. Or you could teach military tactics. Being new to Darlon, and representing a new people, they would line up at your classroom door to listen to you. Just because Darlon is a peaceful planet doesn't mean we aren't prepared to defend ourselves and willing to learn more. You could teach leadership classes too, you certainly have the experience.

"Oh, and to answer your original question, Darlon society works on a credit system. You earn credits as you contribute to society; be it a teacher, artist, musician, writer, any number of things. And there is a limit to the number of credits you can own and any given time, preventing financial greed. Everyone works for the betterment of society and culture. It's actually quite an ingenious system, and its worked for over a thousand years."

After a moment of silence, Ghesh replied, "I – am not sure I have the ability to teach, though your words do peak my interest."

"As a ship commander, didn't you teach your subordinates as they rose through the ranks? Besides, if you still feel uncomfortable, take a class on teaching first. Education is freely available all over Darlon and, as long as you keep your grades high, it's free; you only pay credits if you receive poor grades."

Ghesh smiled, "That certainly would promote diligence in one's studies."

We sat in silence for a time, Ghesh returned to slowly cleaning a balancing modulator arm, obviously lost in thought. His massive hands were surprisingly nimble with even the smallest of parts.

I felt both sad and happy for him at the same time. Sad that the only existence he'd ever known was now over, but happy that he was going to experience a new life, a life without war.

Turns out I was wrong about that last assumption.

5

The reason it takes *Phoenix* longer to reach a destination than a larger ship is due to its smaller jump ring. *Phoenix* can only jump a few light years at a time, then the ring must have time to recharge, which is roughly five hours. Hopefully the research Jhenna and her team were working on would soon help cut this time by half, as well as lengthen the distance of a single jump.

The morning of day two found us roughly a quarter of the way home and in standby mode as the ring repowered. "This is maddning," I commented upon arrival to the bridge. Taking my chair I pulled up reports that had come in overnight. "Jhenna, let's see if we can plan our jumps to arrive near something, anything, so we can have something to do while we wait. If it adds a day to the trip, then so be it."

Jhenna swiveled her chair around. "I'll see what I can do,

Captain, but this sector of space is rather uneventful."

"Surely there's got to be a big rock floating around out there that's just begging to be studied," I said, perhaps a bit too harshly.

Jhenna and I were alone on the bridge as Mr. Or had assumed the night shift for the trip home. She cocked her head slightly as she looked at me. "You seem agitated, Captain."

I looked up from my comm pad, then took a deep sigh. "Sorry, I didn't mean to come across that way. I awoke this morning a bit irritated after a restless night. I feel like we should've accomplished more on Varasay; visited more islands. We traveled a long way for just a few plants, some water samples and a lizard."

My First Officer looked at me for a long moment before speaking. "We can always return at a later time," she said.

I nodded and returned to my morning reports. Mr. Wesh reported that engine number three was only performing at ninety eight percent, but that he expected a full repair today.

Officer Leyt, one of three science officers on board, reported that microbes were found in water puddle samples. They were being frozen for later study.

Officer Wep reported that he was happy no one had touched the lizard with bare hands, it had oils on its skin that that acted like a nerve toxin.

It was reported by Mr. Or that he had nothing to report, that he hoped day shift was a productive one. Mr. Or was indeed a strict protocol man.

Sighing again I returned my comm pad to its little slot, then looked up to find Jhenna still looking at me.

"What?" I asked.

She paused before asking, "Will Captain Narell be assisting you with the zephyr today?"

Shaking my head, I explained, "No, he's working on subspace communiques. Writing letters to his sons and senior commanders explaining his decision to retire are and where we're headed. I imagine the ones to his sons will be difficult."

"I imagine so," Jhenna replied. "I imagine the zephyr is almost complete then? The two of you worked on it most of the day yesterday."

"For the most part, I just need to reinstall the stabilizers."

"Doesn't sound too difficult."

Nodding, I said, "Couple hours worth of work."

"What else needs to be done?"

"Nothing really, except testing it. Not much room on the hanger deck, but I can fly it around a little bit; test some of the maneuvering."

Jhenna swung her chair back around and began, from what I could see, running some safety check protocols. "Sounds like you have a least part of your day occupied then. I'll watch the bridge."

"Thanks," I said. Standing, I turned and left the bridge. It wasn't until I was ten meters down the corridor that I realized I'd been talked right off my own bridge by my First Officer. I had no intentions of working on the zephyr today, but Jhenna had expertly planted the seed. Smiling, I started to turn, but then stopped. "Well played," I said quietly, then headed off to my quarters.

Fifteen minutes later I entered the hanger deck in work clothes. Sitting at the work bench I pulled a stabilizer pad in front of me and opened a small box of tools. This last one needed a few tweaks to its rocker arm, then could be reinstalled with the others.

After tinkering for a while, and a quick self-chastisement, my irritability slowly ebbed away and I gathered back my normally uplifting and happy self; one of the great benefits of keeping the hands and mind busy. Other than the Parakon encounter, the mission, though short, was a success. The *Phoenix* and her crew had performed remarkably and I looked forward to reporting the positive news to DSEA. I also hoped for another mission in the near future, though I would have to find another project to keep me busy if the new voyage was a lengthy one.

The thrum of the engines hummed gently though the steel-deck flooring and kept me company as I worked. The hanger deck was equipped with a music system, but as I had not yet acquired an ear for the types of music on Darlon, the speakers remained silent. Michelle, Yuri and I had brought along some digital music for our trip to Dione, but hadn't been able to bring myself to listen to it yet; I feared the memories would still be too raw.

Though I'm pretty sure all of my memories had returned, they still felt distant, but not so distant as to strike a nerve. During quiet times I would deliberately bring back a memory or two and play with it in my mind; turning them, examining them, reinforcing them. As I sat and worked, and my mood began to recover from the morning, I allowed a memory to float to the surface: My father taking me on my first trip to the moon when I was a child. *Moonbase Ronald Reagan* had just been completed and though most of the compound was for research, part of it was set aside for tourism; a hotel on the moon, so to speak.

The liftoff from Earth terrified me, but once we reached the edge of space and the turbulence stopped, I settled down. The view of Earth outside the hopper-ship's windows captivated me. I'm pretty sure that this view is what set the seed of my future desire to be an astronaut, and one day captain my own ship.

The view from our room was equally breathtaking, but what captivated me even more was the moonwalk. Due to the ultraviolet rays, we were only allowed outside for ten minutes, and even then we were restricted to a fenced area, but still, to stand there and look up at Earth hanging over you like a massive, blue marble was inspiring. I remember looking at my father as he, too, looked up. It was one of the most wonderful memories of my childhood; standing there on the gray-white dust and rock of the moon with my father, and looking up at Earth hovering in the blackness of space.

Little did I know then that just twenty-two years later I would be a captain, and I would have my own ship. My father did not live long enough to see my promotion, having died in a hopper-ship accident when I was just twelve, but I always thought he would have been pretty proud.

My mother, though, did live long enough, not only to see me promoted to Captain Dankin, but also to see me off from Earth before the *Phoenix* mission departed. She was indeed proud and, even though I was in my late twenties, kissed me on the cheek constantly, sometimes right in front of my commanding officers. According to my son's only letter to me, she had still been alive at the time he recorded it. She was frail and well into her eighties, but still thinking clearly. He said she'd never really gotten over the loss of *Phoenix* and spent many evenings rocking on the front porch with a cloth shoulder patch of the *Phoenix* logo in her hand.

These memories rolled around in my mind and I smiled to myself while I worked. I'd listened to my son's letter many times over the months and each time, I felt a little closer to him. His voice and stories were soothing to me. Sometimes I even fell asleep as I played his almost one hour message yet again. I wish it had been even longer, but they had only allowed him sixty minutes, and I was thankful for what I had.

Sometimes I broke down and cried quietly as I listened to the recording, sometimes I smiled and sometimes I laughed. Each time I listened I had no idea how it would affect me, only that it did, and that made me feel human again.

The message also relayed to me that that my son, Terry Jr., was a father, which made me a grandfather. Jodan and Theresa, ages seven and eight respectively, were proud of their 'Grandpa the Space Man', even though they never knew him. Grandpa Terry. I kind of liked that title, better than Captain even.

They were all long gone, of course, but sometimes I liked to think that they weren't, that they were just down the street and I was hearing a comm message from my son.

But we can't exist in the past, and we can't let it control us. But we *can* let it have an influence on our present, we can let it guide us and make us a better person for the future. And make no mistake, I was *way* in the future. So I listened to my son's voice in his missive, and I thought of what my grandchildren must have been like. I did not think of the times that followed the wars on Earth, the wars that decimated the entire planet, that would have

91

accomplished nothing but sorrow and grief. Instead I thought of them as having lived their lives in happiness, surrounded by family and love. I thought of their lives as full and rewarding, though I would never know if that was true.

Many times over the last few months I found myself lost in daydreams about my long ago family. I tried to imagine what my grandchildren looked like, how tall my were, where they liked to vacation, what their favorite books were. What did Terry Jr. look like? Did he have my eyes or Ressa's? Did he have my average brown hair or did he take after Ressa's raven-black locks?

One of the most difficult admissions from my son was that my wife, Ressa, had remarried. "Mom took a long time in getting over the loss of *Phoenix*, over ten years in fact, but she eventually moved on. She remarried about seventeen years ago to a guy named Petershen, an artist from Australia. He's a really great guy and his paintings are highly sought after and – he makes mom happy."

Most times when I heard these few words I smiled, happy that Ressa had found happiness again. But sometimes the emotions got the best of me and I had to wipe tears from my eyes. If we had returned safely from Dione, what would our lives had been like? What would raising a son have been like? Sometimes these questions and others raged through my mind like an out of control wildfire and, at times, I wished my memories had not returned at all.

"Captain?" a voice said, startling me from my thoughts. I looked to my right and found Jhenna standing by my side. I didn't even hear her boots coming down the steel-grate corridor, much less approach my side. I shook my head and looked down at my hands and was startled to see small drops of water on the tabletop. Dropping the tools in my hands I quickly wiped the drops away, though I had no idea why I did such a thing.

Jhenna swung one leg over the bench, straddling the seat, and sat facing me, but I did not look up. She reached and took my right hand in hers and squeezed gently, her other hand went to the base of my neck. She then leaned in closely and rested her head on my shoulder. "Believe me, I understand," she said quietly. She didn't need to say more. Jhenna's struggle with emotions mirrored mine in that we both fought to accept and learn from them. "Remember what you told me a few months ago," she reminded me, "don't let the emotions consume you." I nodded once and returned her hand squeeze.

After a few minutes I felt collected and asked, "Who's watching the bridge?"

"The ship is on autopilot," she replied, lifting her head.

"But – you're the autopilot."

Jhenna smiled. "I know, I'm really good that way." Returning her smile, we both stood and I surprised her with an embrace.

"Thank you," I said, "I needed the company."

She returned the embrace. "I know, I'm good that way too, or at least I'm getting better."

Coeus interrupted my quiet laughter. "Captain?"

Jhenna and I separated. "Yes, Coeus?"

"We have received an emergency sub-space communique from the *Heraway.*"

"And?"

"We are being followed, sir, by a Parakon ship called the *Kloos.*"

"Another scout ship?"

"No, the *Kloos* is a fully armed warship, and, according to my calculations, they will overtake us in less than two days."

N.S. Phoenix

6

As Jhenna and I quickly departed the hanger deck I paged Captain Narell. Grudgingly, I also woke Leiutenants' Or and Wesh as well. "Meet me in the officers lounge," I explained to them. The 'o-lounge', as it was called, was a small room just behind the main bridge and was a rather drab meeting room more than a 'lounge.'

Once everyone was assembled in the small, suffocating room, including a still sleepy-looking Mr. Or, we sat and I called out to Coeus. "Coeus, please repeat what you reported earlier."

"Yes, Captain. We have received an emergency sub-space communique from the *Heraway*. The *Heraway* was finishing repairs when the Parakon ship *Kloos* sub-warped into the system. Captain Brath seems to think they were returning for the scout ship when they discovered it destroyed. The *Kloos* scanned

Varasay and detected the *Heraway*, but seemed to disregard them.

"Captain Brath then noted intense sensor sweeps by the *Kloos* in the area where Phoenix made its first jump. They must have detected the residual energy waves we leave behind after each jump. Captain Brath then noted that the Kloos carefully lined up to match our trajectory, then sub-warped out of the system again.

I looked at Narell. "What does that mean, sub-warp?"

The giant man leaned forward and crossed his arms on the table. "The Kloos is a Keapec-powered ship and capable of generating extraordinary amounts of power. They create a bubble around the ship that effectively isolates them from the fabric of space. It is a dangerous way to travel, one minor mistake and you never return. However, it is highly efficient. The *Phoenix* travels *through* the fabric, a Keapec-powered ship travels *around* it.

"I am familiar with this ship, Captain," Narell continued after a pause, then he looking up at me. "And I am familiar with their commander as well. Commander Vauwent is a shrewd man, and very dangerous. I advise evasive maneuvers, there is nothing *Phoenix* can do against a ship that size."

Thinking for a moment, I instructed the AI, "Coeus, please send a subspace communication back to DSEA and do so every five minutes. The first message should explain our encounter with the *Heraway*, the Parakon scout ship and our current tag-along

96

friends aboard the *Kloos*. Also send all known information concerning the Parakon as well, including the information Captain Narell provided us yesterday."

"Yes, Captain."

"We will not reach Darlon before they overtake us?" I asked Jhenna. She shook her head. "Well," I continued, "we can't very well lead them right to Darlon's doorstep. Is the ring powered up?"

Jhenna pressed a button and a small monitor arose from the table top in front of her. After touching a few buttons, she announced, "We're currently at 98% charge. We can jump now if you wish, but our distance will be shortened."

An idea suddenly surfaced in my mind and I turned to Mr. Wesh. "If I remember correctly we have a spare communications satellite in the cargo hold?"

The thin, bald man nodded. "Yes, and it is in working order."

"Captain," I asked Narell, "How do you trace their ships when they are in sub-warp?"

The Captain nodded, seeming to understand where I was going with this. "You want to release a communications satellite to see if they will follow us, if we change course, or our original trajectory towards Darlon. That makes sense.," he surmised, then paused before continuing. "Like a submarine just under the surface of water, the moving of a Keapec-powered ship creates a disturbance in the spacetime fabric, the bow pushes ripples in the fabric ahead of it. They are hard to locate at times, but it can be done."

"Fine, would you help Mr. Wesh program the satellite to detect these ripples? We'll drop it here as soon as you're ready." The two men started to rise as I asked another question. "Ghesh?" The big man looked down at me. "If there was just one weak spot on the *Kloose*, where would it be?"

The Staelon Captain thought carefully for a moment. "The *Kloose* has three main engines on its stern, each the size of *Phoenix*. Behind the center engine is the main power generator for all three engines.

"I do not advise taking on the Kloose, Captain, you cannot be victorious against them. Even if you fired all weapons aboard *Phoenix* continuously until they are exhausted, would would barely scratch their hull. Gather whatever information you can and send it ahead to your DSEA, let their larger ship come out and meet the *Kloose*. You told me yesterday of the *Classtoria* and I feel positive even Commander Vauwent would second guess taking on a ship that size."

"I don't want to take them on my new-found friend, but if I can slow them down, I will. If they change directions and follow us, then I'm sure we can lose them eventually. But if they continue on towards Darlon –," I sopped and shook my head. "I cannot stand by and do nothing, we have to try. Even if they reach Darlon and do nothing but say hello and leave, they then know where Darlon is, and they'll be back."

I don't know if he saw the look in my eyes, or if I was appealing to his lifetime of commanding warships, but he smiled. "I liked you the moment we met Captain, now I know why," he said, then departed with Mr. Wesh.

"Mr. Or," I said, turning to look into still-sleepy eyes, "please prep the launch sequence. I'm sure the Parakon will destroy the satellite as soon as their sensors find it, make sure it sends a sub-space message to us the moment it knows if the *Kloose* is following us, or heading on to Darlon."

"Yes, Captain," he replied, then stood and made his way to the bridge.

Sitting still and quiet for a moment, I thought deeply through each scenario and what our actions should be, then I looked to Jhenna. "If they continue on to Darlon, I want to open a jump membrane behind the *Kloose*, just like we did on the scout ship. If we take out that engine, we can buy a lot of time."

"But if they stay in sub-warp, we won't be able to do that, Captain. There is no way to fix a target in sub-warp," she explained.

"Then we find a way to peak their curiosity, find a way to

make them stop and come out of warp to investigate."

She thought on this for a moment before coming up with a possible solution. "We could eject one of our engines, then detonate it. The resulting concussion should be big enough to, as you say, peak their curiosity. They'll read the shockwaves first and then, hopefully, follow it to the epicenter. The downside is that we would have to add at least two extra days to get home."

Looking around the starkness that was the o-lounge, I considered Jhenna's option. I also considered the o-lounge could use a facelift, perhaps some happier colors and some paintings on the walls. "So, it'll take us a couple extra days," I said eventually, "but if we strike well, we'll delay them for much longer. I think it's worth the sacrifice."

"Agreed."

"Lets make it happen," I said.

N.S. Phoenix

7

Sub-Lieutenant Ajill was the only one of his race on Darlon, having been awarded the honor of serving in the DSEA by the Higher Learning Council of his home world of Darjering. The competition for such an honor was fierce and Ajill had beat out hundreds of other Senior Educators to be awarded the honor.

The people of Darjering, though spacefaring, were secretive, refusing contact with almost all extraterrestrial life, be they highly intelligent or not. Their existence revolved supremely around education, science, art and shared learning. But they did understand the need for furthering external knowledge and education, hence their assigning one, and only one person every five years to leave the planet and work with other races.

Ajill had now served on Darlon's orbiting communications ring for over four years and his time was growing short, soon he would have to return home. As the fourth year passed he began to contemplate asking for an extension, perhaps for just one more year, but knew it would be rejected by the HLC. It would be time to give someone else an opportunity.

Then he began considering breaking his agreement with the HLC; refusing to leave and seeking permanent residency on Darlon. The only problem with this decision was that HLC may cancel the program altogether, thereby depriving the education for honorees that would follow.

These debates swirled through Ajill's mind as he worked at his desk in the orbiting Communications Ring. His office was called the SSCC, the Sub-Space Communications Command, and his job was to organize, file and forward sub-space communications that were received from deep space exploration ships. He greatly enjoyed his job; hearing about discoveries from all over the galaxy gave him immense pleasure. Just the day before he learned of an aquatic culture on Caressa 5 by the *D.S. Fracalli*. The Ueshe, as they called themselves, lived their entire existence in their planetary oceans and were just on the verge of interstellar space flight with ships that were completely water-filled and capable of half-light speed.

Last week he translated a message from the *D.S. Hombridge* as they'd contacted a race of people called the Meesets who had long ago abandoned their poisoned planet, Huess, due to environmental collapse. They now exclusively lived on massive ships and moons throughout their solar system and were determined to right the wrongs of their history by re-terraforming their own world.

These tidbits of information fascinated Ajill. To think of all these races and civilizations spread throughout the galaxy inspired, captivated and fascinated him.

But in all his years of fascinating reports, he'd never received a hostile or emergency sub-space communique. Ever. So he was a bit surprised when the AI chimed in with a stage one notification.

"Stage One emergency communique from Coeus, AI of *D.S. Phoenix*, channel four-two-four, command line," the AI stated.

Ajill froze for a moment, unsure of what to do exactly. He'd been trained, of course, in what to do when such a communique came through the system, but after four years of having never received one, he was a bit stunned. After a moments hesitation he requested, "AI Orawan, please play the message in its entirety."

Ajill sat as the message played and his eyes grew wide with alarm. When the message had played through he requested an open line to General Commander Jek. "Yes, Lieutenant?" the gruffy commander answered.

"I have received a Stage One emergency communication,

sir. From *Phoenix*. I am forwarding to you now," Ajill explained as he touched several buttons on his comm pad.

Commander Jek listened to the missive and his stern face showed no emotion, but during the playback, he did mutter, "Brilliant, never heard of a jump ring used to do that." Once the recording ended he issued three commands to the young lieutenant. "Issue a fleetwide alert. All ships within two days' travel return to Darlon immediately, including *Classtoria*. Second, contact *Phoenix* and let them know we've received their message and are organizing. Lastly, contact DSEA Fleet Command and forward the message to them as well."

"Yes, Commander."

The comm link was terminated and Ajill executed the Commanders orders. Ajill knew about the Parakon from his studies of Darlonian history. That, and with this new information received from *Phoenix*, Ajill looked out the great window before him at the slowly spinning Darlon, and shuddered.

N.S. Phoenix

8

The ensuing two days found me in a ball of stress, though I did my best to disguise it as we waited for our quarry to catch up with us. We didn't know precisely when the *Kloose* would pass the satellite we'd positioned, so our plans were executed as quickly as possible.

The satellite was programmed to scan for the bow wave ripples in spacetime Captain Narell had described. As soon as it sensed those ripples it would send a communication to a detonation device attached to our ejected engine. The resulting explosion wouldn't be titanic, but it would surely get the attention of the *Kloose* and, it was hoped, it would stop to investigate by coming out of warp. The *Phoenix*, now stationed two hundred kilometers away, would then target their engines.

I had originally thought that if the *Kloose* changed course to follow us, then we'd do our best to lose them, then head home.

But Ghesh changed my mind on that over a glass of triff in the commissary. We sat alone in the darkened room as we discussed what was to come. "Terry," he said, leaning on the table with crossed arms, "I strongly advise taking out their engine whether they change course or not. I do not know for certain, but the last intelligence I had, and this was years ago, is that the *Kloose* has over a hundred of those scout ships you saw. And, as you saw, they are well armed and aggressive. Try to run and lose them and you'll find a hundred scout ships laying a dragnet to sweep you up.

"Even if they do not change course and continue to head towards Darlon, and you take out their primary engine, you will still be kicking the proverbial weekee nest. I'm sure you have a similar insect from your homeworld that would fit that scenario."

Nodding, I said, "Hornets."

Ghesh raised a hand to prove his point. "I advise taking out their engine, then running like hell. Hopefully the damage will immobilize them long enough to send more ships from Darlon to finish the job, and make no mistake, the job must be finished at all costs."

He paused to consider his words before continuing. "Unfortunately, there will be no way to stop them from sending a sub-space distress signal back to their fleet. If that happens, the Parakon will come en-mass."

I had not thought of this contingency, and my mind quickly went to work on the problem. "Well, they must have a transmission array on the ship somewhere. We'd have to first take out the engine, then the array."

Ghesh leaned back in his chair. "I am familiar with the *Kloose*, but not that intimately. But you are right, there must be an array on the outside of the ship somewhere."

We sat quietly for a long while, each lost in our own thoughts. After a few moments, Ghesh suggested a solution. "Though we do not know where the transmission array is, I am familiar with their frequencies. Their array will power up first, then cycle a few times before the transmission is sent. If we can get close enough after firing on their engines, we can scan for that power-up signature, then target the array. We would have roughly a minute before they send the distress call."

But I was shaking my head. "I can't power up the ring three times in a row like that in quick succession. We've enough power to open the the jump membrane once to hit the engine, then again to, as you said, run like hell."

Ghesh lost himself in thought for a while longer. "You have small transport ships in your cargo bay, yes?"

"Souped up zephyrs, yes."

"Are they armed?"

"No, but they could be outfitted with a small laser pulse

cannon. Why?"

"I think Jhenna should be in on this idea," he said with a smile.

Now, a day later, the waiting game continued. Mr. Or tied in the HoloTable to the viewscreen and now he, Jhenna and I watched the abandoned engine float in an infinite field of stars. A few hundred meters away floated our satellite, with a now-armed zephyr hovering next to it.

I touched a comm button. "How are you holding up Ghesh?"

After a pause: "My hindquarters are a bit sore from all this sitting."

I laughed. "Well, hopefully not much longer." I wanted to ask him again if he was sure about this, but refrained.

"However, I must admit," he continued, "that being out here in this tiny ship makes one realize just how small he is in the universe."

"I can well imagine," was my reply.

As we waited, I pulled up the latest communication from DSEA. The *Classtoria*, *Keshkell* and *Drummund* were all fully armed and standing by to jump to our coordinates as soon as *Kloose* was disabled. The original plan was for all three to already be here, but it was feared that the *Kloose* would sense their presence and not come out of warp.

"Captain?" Jhenna called out. I looked up at her. "The satellite is picking up bow waves."

Standing I made a shipwide announcement. "Stand by everyone, things are about to happen very quickly."

I barely spoke my last word when the engine detonated in a small, but blinding explosion. "Ghesh?" I called out to the zephyr.

"Standing by."

Mr. Or widened the viewing field until the explosion was but a small speck in the middle of the viewscreen. Nothing happened for a long moment, then a large area of space seemed to ripple, then glow with a strange reddish hue.

"They're coming out of warp," Ghesh reported, "I'm moving in now."

"Stand by Jhenna, lets unload everything we've got into that engine," I said, moving up behind her chair. She touched numerous controls, then hovered a finger over a single button.

The reddish hue moving through space slowed, then stopped. The transparent red slowly began to intensify as it seemed to ooze from the very fabric of space. Brighter and brighter it became until it was almost blinding, then the light terminated and the *Kloose* was visible. Mr. Or magnified in on it.

"Now!" I said and Jhenna touched the button. Our jump ring sent a spiral of energy into space ahead of us and locked onto a point, then expanded. Before the membrane had fully opened all cannons fired simultaneously. As before, back on Varasay, the Phoenix shuddered as the HyPhos rounds fired and screamed towards the jump membrane.

"Keep firing until we've exhausted the cannons or the engine blows," I instructed. Mr. Or focused in on the stern of the *Kloose* and we watched the shimmering black portal open behind its central engine. It was an immense ship, also scythe-shaped like their smaller scout ships. Lights could be seen on the hull of the almost black ship and the leading front edge was littered with what looked like cannon turrets of some sort. This was indeed a hornets nest, and we were seconds from kicking the hell out of it.

Those seconds passed quickly as our first barrage of HyPhos rounds emerged as if by magic behind the *Kloose* and impacted their desired target. The result was immediate as the central engine became a blinding ball of light as it exploded.

Jhenna launched another salvo and the affect was equally devastating.

"Approaching *Kloose* now," Ghesh reported.

"I give it a less than a minute for them to realize they didn't have an engine failure and that they're under attack."

"Agreed, scanning the surface now."

It was quite obvious that a third salvo was not needed, The exploding engine rent the engine blast cone into twisted, white-hot shreds. The explosion was so powerful that the *Kloose* was now gently slewing sideways.

Seconds ticked by at an agonizing pace. Jhenna reduced the size of the jump membrane from roughly three hundred meters to two, just enough room for a zephyr to enter.

"Their sensor sweeps just located us, Captain." Jhenna Reported.

"That did it!" Ghesh voice came over the comm system. "Their sensor and communications array are the same, I see it ahead. I'm Going in!"

Mr. Or focused in and we watched Ghesh as he brought the zephyr in over the dark gray skin of the *Kloose*. He weaved maddeningly around towers, gun turrets and other strange protrusions from the hull of the massive ship.

"I'm picking up a transmission power up signature," said Jhenna.

Ghesh responded, "I read it, almost there!"

He darted up, down, left and right in his furious flight to the array. I'm quite sure a zephyr had never been piloted in such a manner. And probably never would again.

"I'm there, firing now!"

We watched the viewscreen as Ghesh fired both laser pulse cannons. White beams of laser light erupted and impacted the array tower in a direct hit and the tower exploded in a massive ball of twisted metal and flaming pieces of flying debris.

"Ahh!" Ghesh yelled over the comm.

"What is it?" I called in return.

"The zephyr's been hit by the debris! I'm loosing power!"

I quickly said to Jhenna, "Move the membrane to intercept him." Jhenna nodded and began furiously tapping the keyboard in front of her.

Mr Or called out from the back of the bridge. "Better hurry, he's being pursued!" I looked up to the viewscreen to see what looked like a modified version of a *Kloose* scout ship, but this one was bristling with what were obviously weapons, and they were all glowing with full charge. It too was flying close to the surface of the mother ship, dodging this way and that as it closed the distance on Ghesh.

Meanwhile Jhenna was moving the membrane as quickly as possible to intercept. It was going to be close. "Ghesh!" Jhenna said aloud, "keep as straight a course as you can and I'll scoop you out!"

"The faster the better!" The zephyr still had some power, but it was noticeably limping along. Finally though, Jhenna had the membrane directly in front of Ghesh, but not before the pursuing ship fired its weapons. The zephyr took a direct hit as it penetrated the membrane and arrived two hundred meters in front of *Phoenix*.

"Ghesh!" I called out. No answer. "Ghesh!? I called again. Still no answer. "Lieutenant Wesh," I called down to the hanger deck, "take the other zephyr and go get him!"

"Already suiting up sir!"

Then things went from bad to worse. Right as Jhenna terminated the jump membrane, the nose of the pursuing ship had penetrated it, effectively cutting the ship in half. Now, as we looked in horror, the pointed front end of that ship was bearing down on us.

"Evasive maneuvers!" I called out. Jhenna quickly grabbed control stick and pulled backward and to the left. The *Phoenix* thrusters responded immediately as the ship lurched backward.

But it was too late, the roughly twenty meter section of the ship was moving too fast. Reverse thrusters were not powerful enough to avoid the collision. The section impacted the leading edge of *Phoenix's* left wing. The impact was lessened slightly due to us moving backward, but the concussion slammed *Phoenix* into a spin. Anything not tied down on the bridge went airborne, including me.

After traveling three meters through the air and crashing down to the hard, steel floor, emergency alarms sounded. Quickly gaining my feet, and helping Mr. Or to his, I called to Jhenna, "Did that breech the hull?" I shouted over the alarms.

After a pause, "No breech!" she responded and fought to regain control of *Phoenix*. Checking myself for bodily damage, I made my way back to my chair. Some bruises were defiantly in my near future, but at least nothing was broken. I silenced the alarms and said to Jhenna, "Let's get out of here, anywhere but near that hornets nest."

After a moment of initiating commands, she stopped and turned to look at me with wide eyes. "The jump ring is inoperable, it must have sustained an impact as well."

I touched a comm button. "Mr Wesh! Do you have Captain Narell? We need to be out of here!"

"On our way back, sir! He's unconscious, but alive!"

"Captain!" Mr. Or cried out. "They're launching more of those ships!" I looked to the viewscreen and, as predicted, after we kicked the nest, the hornets were emerging.

To Jhenna I said, "The second they're on board, engage both engines, full power –," but I never finished my sentence. Suddenly we were no longer alone with the *Kloose*. Three massive jump membranes erupted in the vicinity of the Kloose and the *Classtoria*, *Keshkell* and *Drummund* slowly emerged into our little war-torn sector of space.

Before the ships even completed their emergence from their respective membranes they opened fire. The devastation was immediate and terrifying. The outer hull of the two kilometer-long *Kloose* erupted in explosions from stem to stern in a highly choreographed attack. The smaller ships that had emerged from the enemy vessel immediately terminated their pursuit of *Phoenix* and turned their attention to the newly arrived threat.

But even for them, it was too late. Smaller combat ships with their own jump rings poured from the hangers of *Classtoria* and the *Drummund* in a vicious swarm. Rings of fire erupted from their jump rings and the smaller enemy vessels vanished in white balls of fire.

"We're safely aboard, Captain!" Mr. Wesh announced.

But Jhenna made no move to engage the engines. The devastation being wrought upon the *Kloose* kept our eyes locked upon the viewscreen. Such an onslaught I had never witnessed before, and hoped to never see again. The attack was overwhelming, decimating and complete. Even after ten minutes, when the *Kloose* was breaking apart into fiery hulks of half-molten chunks of metal, the attack continued. HyPhos cannons, laser pulse cannons and compressed hydrogen cannons fired at will and the *Kloose* lit up like a small sun. Though I could not tell precisely, I don't believe the *Kloose* was able to return fire in any way, so complete was the overwhelming force.

On and on the decimation continued. Massive cannon turrets on all three DSEA ships began to glow white hot as they wrought carnage. All three ships were through their respective membranes now, their jump rings powered down, and yet the obliteration continued.

It went on for another ten minutes until the remains of the *Kloose* were nothing but scattered fragments of unrecognizable scraps of steel. There were a few more *Kloose* attack ships to chase down, but eventually they too succumbed to the DSEA total annihilation.

It was clear to me. This was not just overreaction, this was a message. A message to the Parakon, should they ever discover the remains. A message of extreme warning.

When it was over, and the three new arrivals ceased fire, I sat back in my Captain's chair and, I think for the first time in almost five minutes, took a breath. I don't know how long I sat and watched the now calm viewscreen, but I was eventually brought around by a page from Dr. Yent. "Captain?"

Shaking my head at the carnage I'd just witnessed, I opened a connection to our small sick bay. "Yes?"

"I have Captain Narell in my care, sir. He has regained consciousness and should be fine. At least he says he will, as I am not familiar with his biology. I have, however, insisted that he stay under my care, at least for the next twenty hours."

"Thank you, Doctor," I said, and terminated the link.

I stood and walked to Mr. Or's station. "Are you alright?" I asked.

The science officer nodded. "Just a few bumps and scratches," he said, then paused with a shake of his head. "I must say, Captain, these last few days have been – shall we say – intriguing, to say the least. As a man of science, it is difficult to witness such violence and destruction."

Reaching up to pat him gently on the shoulder, I said, "That makes two of us Mr. Or." We stood quietly for a moment as we watched the three DSEA ships hover over the holotable. The *Classtoria*, the flagship of the DSEA, was by far the biggest of the three. The smaller *Keshkell* and *Drummund*, though also exploration vessels, doubled as defense ships. They looked similar to the Classtoria's arrowhead shape, but differed with their wide fins that rose high above the upper deck. These were filled with cargo bays that housed DSEA's small fighter ships called *warlons*.

Warlons were of a flying-wing design, but their wings curled severely back underneath the main body. They were extremely agile both in the vacuum of space and in atmosphere. Mr. Or and I watched as, one by one, they returned to their respective ships.

"Captain?" Jhenna called. I turned to the front of the bridge. "Commander Ballon is hailing us." I nodded and made my way to the viewscreen as Jhenna patched him through. His marvelously bald and tattooed head soon appeared. He reached up and tapped his lower lip with a huge finger while trying to look confused.

"Now I admit I'm getting older, and my memory isn't what it used to be, but this seems familiar in some way, yes?"

The first smile I'd had all day crept upon my lips. "I have no idea what you're talking about, Commander. Perhaps Dr. Bastra can prescribe you some memory pills?"

The Commander returned my smile. "Captain Dankin! Out here trying to start a galactic war? What has gotten into you? I thought we'd trained you better than this! Mr. Or!" he said, looking at my borrowed science officer. "How could you let this happen?"

Both Mr. Or and I ignored his banter as I informed him, "Our jump ring was damaged. We could use a lift."

Nodding, he looked at Jhenna. "First Officer Jhenna, bring her on in, we'll leave the door open for you," he instructed, but then looked back at me, "oh, and Captain Dankin?"

"Yes?"

With those smiling, honest eyes, he said, "Well done."

\* \* \*

Within thirty minutes Jhenna had guided us to the main hanger deck of *Classtoria* and most of the crew had departed.

Ghesh, however, had elected to stay in the small *Phoenix* sickbay. He didn't want the first day of his new life to be in a major hospital ward. Dr. Yent obliged and agreed to stay on duty until his twenty-hour observation was complete.

Two hours later, after I finished filing reports, I arrived in sickbay. I had a small box in one hand, a liter of trill in the other, and two small glasses squeezed between my arm and ribs. Ghesh watched me enter and place the glasses and bottle on a nearby table, then pull a chair next to his bed. "Thought you could use a drink," I stated.

"Thank you, Captain," he replied, not looking too happy about being in a bed.

I held up the small box. "In the short time I've known you, you come across as a man who really dislikes being singled out and paraded around like a hero."

Ghesh smiled around some bandaged and lengthy lacerations across his face. They didn't look bad, but must have hurt like hell. "You would be correct in that assessment."

"I figured as much, that's why I talked DSEA out of a formal award ceremony when we return to Darlon." I flipped open the box and showed him the contents.

"What is this?"

"It's the DSEA medal for bravery in the line of duty," I explained as he took it from my hand. "You put yourself in harms

119

way for this ship, for a people you don't even know. Thank you."

The big man offered a small smile and a nod. "You're welcome," he said, then closed the box. "How about that drink now?"

Obliging, I stood, poured two drinks and, returning to the bed, handed him one.

We sat, drank and talked late into the night.

*Afterword*

All evidence pointed to the Kloose failing to issue a distress call back to their fleet, though it was assumed that at some point their absence would be noticed and a mission would be sent to find them. As I was only a lowly, and rookie, starship captain, I was not involved with the talks as they progressed about what to do if the Parakon eventually found Darlon.

But that was fine by me. It had been almost two months since our run-in with the Parakon and I was in no rush to meet them again. Phoenix had been repaired and was on standby, but no new missions had been issued yet, so my ship was docked in orbit, empty and locked up, waiting for her next mission. Mothballed, so to speak.

In the meantime, I'd been occupying myself with taking

*classes at a nearby university, one on philosophy and another on basic mechanical skills in repairing engines and weapons that were common in the DSEA fleet. After recent events, and Captain Narell's words of wisdom:* "When one's ship is damaged in battle, it behooves one to know how to fix things, and very quickly I might add," *I decided to learn as much as possible in mechanics and engineering.*

*And I certainly didn't want to have my pashtak blown to smithereens.*

*Speaking of Narell, during the first week after our return he was officially given the titles of Commander Emeritus and Staelon Ambassador to Darlon. He began taking an assortment of classes at DSEA and, although he was not required to do so, began teaching a few as well, mainly revolving around battle tactics and defense.*

*"I never knew how agreeable it would be to me to teach such eager minds," he said to me over a comm link one evening. His facial lacerations had healed, but he now sported two long scars across his face, making him look even more intimidating. "And you were correct, they literally line up at my door, my classroom is standing room only."*

*He had taken a residence roughly ten kilometers south of my home. We met often for and afternoon of fishing in the bay below my house, or just to have a glass of trill. Our friendship grew to one of great and mutual respect.*

*Another relationship continued to grow for me as well; the one between Jhenna and myself. I suppose, in a way, it was inevitable. Despite the human ancestors we'd rescued on the moon all those months ago, Jhenna was still the closest person to me, in a sense I could not quite put my finger on.*

*Though I was initially uncomfortable several months ago, I'd become more and more comfortable with letting Ressa go and entering a new relationship. I accepted that I would always miss my wife, but it came a point where I understood that I had to move on. I'm sure Ressa would have agreed, even if it was a relationship with an sentient machine, even though I didn't see her that way.*

*Jhenna came over as often as she could, when work didn't detain her in orbit. Her work with the other AI's was breaking ground in a whole new field of mathematics and, as of a week prior, she was elected to the senior board position of their group. They eventually agreed that her advanced emotions gave her an edge to problem solving, and Jhenna was thrilled.*

*As I sat in my living room, enjoying a day off and thinking over these last two months, I could not help but smile. I was excited about the future and what it may hold. But my smile was interrupted as I heard the approach of a zephyr, but I quickly identified the particular engine sound belonging to Jhenna's custom zephyr. After mine was complete, she decided she wanted one as well; orange with red accents.*

*I heard the zephyr dock, then boots across the porch, then the door open and close. As my back was to the door, I rolled my head back to look up, and soon Jhenna came into view. She put her hands on my shoulders, leaned down and kissed me.*

*"Hey you," she said.*

*"Hey to you, too."*

*I rose and embraced her and after a moment, and some batting of eyelashes, we started to head to the bedroom, but we never made it.*

*"Captain?" came the voice of Coeus.*

*I closed my eyes. "Yes?"*

*"I have received a missive from DSEA."*

*I looked at Jhenna. "And?"*

*"The Phoenix is being assigned a new mission, your presence is required immediately at DSEA command."*

*I sighed. Jhenna made a pouty face.*

Authors Note

Though there are no solid plans as of yet for a third *Phoenix* book, I thought I'd leave the ending open. You know, just in case!

As before, this second book was also based on numerous rewrites of an original book called the Black Divide, a book I began over eight years ago. *Phoenix, Part One* took almost six months to complete, while *Phoenix, Part Two* came pouring out in just over two months. Writing is always easier once you've gotten to know your characters and, in many ways, my characters wrote a majority of the words. I was just here to punch little, square keys on my keyboard.

I hope you have enjoyed *Phoenix, Part Two,* as I had a blast writing it. The time now has come to finally rewrite a book I started three years ago called 'Rider: The Imminence.' Not quite science fiction, not quite action-adventure, not quite fantasy, yet all three at the same time. The book currently stands at sixty-five thousand words and is written in third person, but I've decided to slim it down and rewrite it in first person. I love writing in first person, you can become much more intimate with your character that way.


## A Note About Self Publishing


With the recent advent of Websites such as Smashwords, Wordclay and CreateSpace, the door has swung wide open to anyone who wants to publish a book. No red tape, no publishing house hurdles to clear, no rejection letters, no fat-cat publisher who looks at you and your work and only sees dollar signs. Though I do have to pay a fee for every book that I sell through CreateSpace, I can _sell_ _my_ _book_, not fight with hurdles and red tape.

There is one common drawback to self-published books though, the editing is not always so great. As doctors make the worst patients, authors make the worst editors. Me included.

It's not that budding, self-publishing authors don't _want_ have their books professionally edited, it's that most of us can't _afford_ to have it done. The average charge to have a book professionally edited hovers around five cents a word. That means I would have had to shuck out thirteen-hundred dollars to have _Phoenix, Part Two_ edited, and guess what I don't have?

You guessed it.

So I have to edit myself, or implore family and friends to help; family and friends who have busy lives of their own; work, kids, mortgage payments, school, a car that needs a new tire, a lawn to mow, a weekend Honey-Do list; you get the picture.

So while I encourage you to buy books from budding, self-publishing authors, I ask that you forgive them their minor editing issues. They're only human and, most of them, really just write for the sheer joy of writing, not to have the Editor Police chase them down every step of the way.

I and my fellow self-publishers would appreciate it.


MDS

26 Feb. 2013